Pra

MW01281889

From Diane Frank, a beautiful love story from the dream world, where humans and mermaids meet. In her masterful lyrical style, this poet musician takes us on a journey through realms of water, music, passion and art. As we follow the lives of a family of creative souls, we feel the flow of the sacred feminine, orchestrating and guiding at every turn. A gift from a master of light and dreams, *Mermaids and Musicians* speaks to the artist, musician, poet and dreamer in all of us.

    —Jennifer Read Hawthorne, co-author, #1 New York
    Times bestseller *Chicken Soup for the Woman's Soul*;
    author, *A Canopy of Stars: Poems*

"One of the best ways to learn about humans is to listen to their songs." Every chapter in *Mermaids and Musicians* sings. With exquisite language, Diane Frank weaves joy and heartbreak, community and loneliness, surrealism and realism into a novel of hope. This delectable book uproots readers from the Appalachian Mountains and transports them to the Pacific coast, following the dreams of various characters, all of them artists and musicians, all believers that this wild, precious earth is worth saving. Frank delights in every color and sound, every magical moment we sometimes forget as we traverse from childhood into adults. This is a book I would devour first, then go back and luxuriate in the second, third, and subsequent readings. A must read for anyone who longs to return to a world of compassion and beauty.

    —KB Ballentine, author of *Almost Everything,*
    Almost Nothing; and *Spirit of Wild*

Mermaids and Musicians is a feast for the senses, the images conjuring sights, sounds and tastes that metamorphosize into larger concepts. When Diane Frank introduces music into her novel, it takes on a depth, both joyful and painful, that is, in my opinion, her finest work. Bravo!

—Jill Rachuy Brindel, Cellist, San Francisco Symphony

Diane Frank has that amalgam of poetry and prose just right. Her language has perfect pitch. It's a knockout.

—Robert Scotellaro, author of *Measuring the Distance* and *What We Know So Far*

Diane Frank's *Mermaids and Musicians* is full of magic – not the ordinary magic of impossible feats, rather the more delicious kind, that sets up residence in our souls. I love the way poetic passages leap out at me, then sink gracefully back into the narrative.

—Anya Luz Lobos, author of *Wild Knowing*

Mermaids and Musicians

A Novel

Diane Frank

1st WORLD
PUBLISHING

Mermaids and Musicians
Diane Frank

Published by 1st World Publishing
P.O. Box 2211, Fairfield, Iowa 52556
tel: 641-209-5000 • fax: 866-440-5234
web: www.1stworldpublishing.com

First Edition

ISBN: 978-1-4218-3686-7

LCCN: Library of Congress Cataloging-in-Publication Data

Diane Frank
PO Box 150300
San Rafael, CA 94915

Email: GeishaPoet@aol.com

Website: www.dianefrank.com

Cover Art: "Bed of Roses" painted by Victor Nizovtsev
"Bed of Roses" © by Victor Nizovtsev.

Book Design: Rodney Charles and Anuj Mathur

Waves of appreciation to everyone who shared their musical gifts to
help me bring this book into being, especially Jill Rachuy Brindel,
Amos Yang, Hannah Scarborough, Annie Rodier Turano,
James MacQueen and Bernard Chevalier. Blessings to Barbara
Newell, Robin Lim, Melanie Gendron and Orion Hawthorne
for sharing their vision. Blessings to the poets and musicians on
Signal Mountain, especially KB Ballentine and Jim Canestrari,
who shared their home and took me hiking every evening. Special
thanks to Erik Ievins, Anya Luz Lobos, Elinor Gale, and Rodney
Charles for great suggestions and careful proofreading.

For everyone who gave me music

Contents

On Signal Mountain

The Cove by Anchor Bay

The Prophesy Stones

Mermaids
and Musicians

"Some Mermaids possess powers of prophecy,
and all have the ability to protect their loved ones from harm.
They can also bring bad luck,
and even great catastrophe, to any who betray them."

– H. Bowen

On Signal Mountain

Chapter 1:

Halfway up Signal Mountain

Close to the Cumberland Trail on Signal Mountain, rhododendron and mountain laurel were blooming in the forest. Something about the Appalachian Mountains called to him. Life had shuffled an unexpected change of plans, and he needed a new beginning. Thirty-two years old, healthy and strong, it was not too late to start over. Daniel could communicate with birds by telepathy, and he knew the birds would tell him where to land. Crawling out of his tent that morning, he saw a cardinal – chattering red ball of fire – streak the early morning air and land on a catalpa tree nearby. The bird was just beyond his reach but close enough to see clearly. The cardinal kept singing, and that was the signal he had been waiting for.

A few days later, he rented a cabin partway up the mountain – a rustic split timber shelter formerly used by forest rangers and then expanded with screens and walls.

The kitchen was in an enclosed porch on the side of the cabin, with an antique stove, a porcelain sink, shelves for dishes on the wall, and a built-in spice cabinet. Daniel stowed his sleeping bag and pillow in the loft. Yes, he would live here for a while, but his soul kept guiding him further up the mountain. Every time he hiked on the Cumberland Trail, he felt his cares and worries drop away. The leaves were exotic, some of them shaped like handprints of mythical animals. He loved the way sunlight touched them in the morning, lighting the leaves as if from inside. Bluebirds, wrens, nuthatches, and finches built nests in trees close to the trail. Flitting across the trail as he hiked, so many species of exotic butterflies – Tawny Emperor, Painted Lady, Tiger Swallowtail, Great Spangled Fritillary. Hummingbirds darted and dove to wildflowers – whoosh of green slicing the air. The mountain air was cool in the early morning, hot and humid as the sun rose higher.

After a week of hiking in the mountains, he drove back to Memphis in his blue Chevy pickup to gather the things he loved from the life he had left behind. Everything else, he left on the sidewalk next to the Salvation Army, with three bags of groceries for the homeless community. The next morning, he packed his truck carefully for the drive to his new home, with a trailer hitched behind to carry the furniture. One of his neighbors helped him load the trailer. Before leaving, he walked through his empty house with a flood of memories, then locked the front door and drove away. East of Memphis, the road was flat for a while, then climbing to small hills, then winding through Appalachian mountain roads until he reached Chattanooga. As he was driving, he listened to Bela Fleck and Edgar Meyer and hummed along with them. *Uncommon Ritual*, the theme for the first part of his journey. Then *Music for Two*, recorded live in Nashville during a concert. A dream and a promise. Something about those low notes and their weave with the banjo thrilled him.

Back on Signal Mountain, Daniel unpacked his truck and filled his cabin with musical instruments. Four violins, a banjo, a viola, a cello and a bass fiddle in the living room. A box of recorders, two flutes, two clarinets, an oboe, a bassoon, two French horns, two trumpets, two trombones and a tuba in the closet. Lots of percussion, enough for a room full of small children. His furniture, gifts from his grandmother, all hand-crafted by wood-workers who lived in the mountains – a maple dresser, a mirror inside a carved frame, an oak kitchen table with four Shaker chairs, and a maple bed he hoped to share one day. Since he felt powerfully drawn to this place, he knew that love would be waiting somewhere. His grandmother told him that every human, like every bird and butterfly, has a soulmate. When he was a boy, she told him stories about fireflies lighting the way for fairies and children lost in the forest. While she was still on the earth, she made him a wedding quilt – a pattern of interconnected rings in turquoise, fuchsia and forest green, with patches of but-terflies, leaves and flowers. A blessing and a promise. He put the quilt on his bed, even though he was still waiting.

The mountain schools needed a music teacher, so he was hired in September. Daniel had tremendous patience with children and asked them to listen carefully to the sounds when he showed them how to find the notes. He always had them sing and match his pitches before the instruments came out. As they progressed, many of his students joined the orchestra and the band and gave concerts twice a year. Students learning the violin and cello used the Suzuki books and learned classical technique, but on Fridays, he'd tell them to put the books away, and by ear, he taught them fiddle tunes. Their reward, when the tune was memorized, was to have their teacher take out his bass and play with them.

Sometimes he took them hiking up the mountain to hear how music sounds in the open air. He'd ask them to listen to the sounds of the birds and the wind, then fill the trails with harmony. Music in nature waves out to the leaves, flies with the birds, and swirls into the sky. The young musicians hiked behind their teacher, his dark hair woven with a bit of silver, muscles strong from hiking since he was a boy and canoeing in the rivers that snaked through Tennessee. Daniel was a large man, someone you could see lumbering up a mountain in the company of bears and loblolly pines.

Every Friday night, Daniel went to the Mountain Opry to listen to bluegrass and fiddle tunes. Sometimes he'd bring a banjo and sometimes a violin. On the last Friday of the month, a few of his students went with him. Backstage, you could hear musicians jamming in practice rooms, forming ensembles shortly before taking the stage. A new group came on stage every thirty minutes, with Mountain People flat-foot clogging in front of the band. In the audience, you could see toe tapping grandparents sharing the music they loved with their wide eyed grandchildren. Veteran pickers shared the stage with the next generation of young musicians learning traditional fiddle tunes by ear, along with recently composed tunes that gathered countermelodies with each new player joining in. Liquor and tobacco were prohibited, but harmony was everywhere.

After a night at the Opry, Daniel drove back to his cabin humming the new tunes he learned, scat singing and weaving harmonies. Music was his path through the mountains. Music was his joy. Music floated through his dreams.

Chapter 2:

The Dance Barn

*D*aniel played banjo and fiddle with local musicians every Friday night at the Mountain Opry. He went to barn dances on the mountain when he could, as he came from a family of dancers and musicians. Soon after he was born, his parents took him to dances in the baby basket, and by the time he was six years old, he was out on the floor with the other dancers. His parents gave him a violin as soon as he was old enough to hold a bow, and the old time fiddlers taught him their favorite tunes. He often woke up with music in the morning, and by the time he was eight years old, he was sharing his tunes with the older fiddlers. Music was in his soul and in his bones.

Signal Mountain had a barn dance on the third Saturday of each month, in a red barn with a dance floor and a fiddle painted on the silo. Sometimes he played with the band, but he always spent part of the evening on the dance floor. The caller had a long list of favorite contras and squares, and just before the break, the musicians sped up the tempo for flat-foot clogging.

In October of his second year on the mountain, Daniel noticed a woman he hadn't seen before. He was on the stage, playing bass with an old time band called Half Moon Strutters, when he saw a flash of red hair flying around a dancer with a very inventive style. From that moment, he watched her as he played. She was deeply tuned to the music and let it move through her. Her smile was sweet and her skirt, a patchwork of jewel tones, twirled in waves around her as she danced. Now in the back of the hall. Now twirling and coming up the line. Just before break, she walked in front of the stage to join the Mountain People flat-foot clogging. Maybe it was her long red hair or maybe the way she danced, but he couldn't take his eyes off her.

During the break, the hosts served two kinds of soup and cornbread, with apple pie and a few treats from the dancers. Daniel ate with the band and kept his distance, but when it was time to dance again, he walked onto the dance floor instead of the stage. The woman he had been watching was standing by herself, so he asked her to dance. She smiled and took his hand, so they partnered for a square dance and later, for a waltz. Her wavy red hair fell in rivers almost to her waist. Her soulful green eyes sparkled like pools of mountain water. Eyes that gazed so deeply into his that he felt she already knew his secrets.

That night after he went home, Daniel couldn't stop thinking about her. *I wonder where she is. I wonder who she is. I wonder if I will ever see her again.*

Two days later, Daniel woke up with a new waltz in the

morning. Silently, he dedicated it to her, even though he didn't know her name. He drove to school humming the tune, and before he went inside, wrote it with a Palomino Blackwing pencil on music notation paper. During his break, he went to the piano and started experimenting with chords. Daniel liked to use chords that were somewhat unpredictable. They always fit the music but pulled his emotions in unexpected directions. On Friday, which was always Mountain Music day, he taught his young musicians to play the waltz, and they improvised with the chords. After working it for a while, Daniel gave them a smile and a nod, and brought out his bass – the signal they were waiting for. As they played, he felt the room fill with the spirit of the woman he hoped to see again.

He thought about her every night before he fell asleep, wondering when he would dance with her again. In his dreams, a flash of red hair flying. Those beautiful green eyes. From somewhere deep inside, he felt he knew her. A month later, on the third Saturday, she came to the dance barn again. This time, Daniel asked her for a contra, hoping that he would measure up to her expectations. His worries had nothing to do with reality, as various partners had praised his dance style for years. As a musician, his timing was always perfect. He was skilled in all of the figures, and he knew how to lead his partner gently into a twirl without being late for the next figure. He noticed how responsive she was to his lead. She met his gaze and she was always smiling. At the end of the dance, he did a gentle lean toward the music, and she leaned into his hip with her left foot lifted gracefully to her knee.

At the break, they found seats next to each other to

enjoy the mid-dance snack – soup and cornbread. They were both silent, but at one point, she got up and brought back two slices of pumpkin pie.

He thanked her and said, "Hey, my name is Daniel. I moved to Signal Mountain two summers ago. I was out here hiking and fell in love with the mountain."

She smiled and said, "I'm Lucinda. I grew up here."

"Maybe you can show me some of places on the mountain I haven't discovered yet."

"I'd enjoy that. By the way, I like your style on the bass, and I think I've heard you play fiddle and banjo at the Mountain Opry. How many instruments do you play?"

"Oh, probably most of them. I started with the fiddle when I was maybe four. My first teachers were old time musicians in Memphis, and later, they taught me to play banjo and bass. Then, at the university, if you want to teach, you learn all of the instruments in an orchestra and a band. I teach music at both elementary schools on Signal Mountain. Four days a week, we have music classes, band and orchestra. On Fridays, we close the music books and I teach them fiddle tunes. Once a month, I take my best students to the Mountain Opry and we play one of the sets."

"I know I've seen you there a few times. I've been going to the Mountain Opry with my grandparents since I was a girl. Grandpa passed on a few summers ago, so Grandma and I take care of the house and the vegetable garden now. We sew and weave together. It's something we've been doing since I was eight."

"Everyone should have a Grandma like that!"

"Grandma is a master quilter. It's a family tradition.

We make quilts, skirts, dresses, and weavings to hang on the wall. I bring them to galleries in Chattanooga."

The band was back on stage, playing a hambo, and then the caller asked everyone to take partners for a contra. Daniel and Lucinda walked onto the dance floor holding hands. As the band played "Round the Horn" and then "Julia Delaney," they moved in harmony, as if connected by telepathy. When he asked her to waltz with him at the end of the evening, she smiled and accepted. Their waltz was sweet, and she kept eye contact with him the whole time. At the end of the waltz, he led her into a gentle dip. Then pulled her up into a pivot twirl.

In December, Daniel played with the band, but he sat with Lucinda during the break. More gentle conversation. Before he went back on the stage, he told her, "Pay attention to the waltz at the end of the evening. I wrote it – it's called 'Lucinda.'" Her eyes went wide.

During the waltz, even though she was dancing with someone else, she kept looking at the stage. Then, because it was a holiday dance, the caller told the dancers to take partners for a second waltz. Daniel walked off the stage to waltz with Lucinda. They waltzed with pivot turns at the end of each long phrase, and he led her into a graceful dip during the last chord of the waltz. By the end of the evening, they felt a chord between them that they couldn't quite articulate. The chord kept humming in their dreams.

In January, the dancers were forming carpools for the Valentine's Dance in Knoxville and making arrangements to stay with friends. Daniel asked Lucinda if she was going. She said, "I'd like to, although I haven't gone to a dance weekend before."

"That sounds like a yes?"

"Yes, but I've never been to a dance beyond Signal Mountain."

"Dancers from all over the Midwest and the South will be coming to Knoxville for the weekend. They have two bands, some of the best dance musicians I know. Local dancers put out a potluck for lunch and we go in groups for dinners. It's a great way to get to know the people you dance with. I can make the arrangements for both of us. I'll make sure we'll be riding in the same car and staying at the same house."

"I've seen flyers for those dances but it always felt like too far to drive."

"There's a tribe of contra dancers who meet up every few weeks at dance weekends. If you do the drive with a group of friends, the time passes quickly. And the best part – I'll have lots of time to dance with you!"

Daniel walked her to her car after the dance and gave her a hug. A long slow hug, which made her feel warm inside.

On the Friday before Valentine's Day, their group met at the dance barn in the early afternoon and chose carpools based on where they would be hosted. Half the group would be staying in a large Victorian house owned by one of the local dancers. Daniel and Lucinda were in that group. The others brought sleeping bags and rented a motel room close to the dance. For the next few hours, they drove on winding mountain roads until they arrived in Knoxville. For most of the drive, they listened to CDs of contra dance bands and a Kitka CD with Bulgarian music.

The dance was huge – more than two hundred dancers

with six contra lines. The Latter Day Lizards played the first half of the dance, followed by a waltz. Then, the Moving Violations took over the stage. Daniel and Lucinda agreed to find each other every three or four dances the first night, along with the last waltz. By Saturday night, they were doing every other dance together, and of course, the last waltz.

When they got back to their host's home at midnight, he served ice cream and blueberry muffins in the kitchen. The classical music station was airing some gorgeous music, starting with "Mysterious Mountain" by Alan Hovhaness, followed by "The Lark Ascending" by Ralph Vaughan Williams. Everyone was too excited to go to sleep, so they stayed up talking and listening for a while. Eighteen dancers were staying at the house, some in bedrooms, some on sofas, and some in sleeping bags on the floor. One by one, they disappeared into their dreams.

The Sunday dance started at 10:00 in the morning and went until mid-afternoon. The Moving Violations played the first half of the dance, with their twin fiddle grooves. Then, the Latter Day Lizards played the rest of the dance. After dancing for three days, everyone was in an altered state of consciousness, filling the floor with circles, stars and swirls until the last waltz. Both bands were selling their CDs from the stage and they were swarmed by dancers. Then it was time to go. The Signal Mountain dancers were excited to play their new Latter Day Lizards CD as they drove, and they stopped at a Catfish Shack for dinner.

Daniel and Lucinda started seeing each other more often after that. Sometimes a hike in the mountains.

Sometimes a dinner or a movie. Sometimes a ride down the mountain to the museum, a concert, or art galleries in Chattanooga. Daniel woke up with music more and more often now. He kept music notation paper next to his bed. Whenever he saw Lucinda, he always had a new waltz or contra tune to share.

Chapter 3:

Fog Melting under Sunlight

*E*ven with the excitement of new love and the quiet joy they felt when they were together, it took them a while to believe it. Daniel and Lucinda each had stories of lovers who had made big promises they were not able to keep, including a broken engagement. It was hard to trust again after such a huge disappointment.

As they were piecing together a quilt, Lucinda told her grandmother, "Daniel is different from other men I've met. I know that from deep inside. I want to trust him, but I can't rush into things."

Grandma agreed, "No need to hurry. I knew your Grandpa for a year before we married."

"I'm not sure I want to get married."

"No need to decide right now. My life with your Grandpa was a blessing for many years. As you know, it was hard the last year, after he became ill. I still miss him every day. This might sound funny, but I talk to him every night before I go to sleep."

"Does he answer?"

"He visits me in my dreams."

They went back to working on the quilt – a pattern called "Star of the Bluegrass" they had seen in a museum, stitching diamond-shaped fabric pieces together to make an eight-pointed star. They worked with calico fabrics in carefully selected shades of green, blue and purple, with tiny flowers in contrasting colors.

Grandma leaned back in her chair, then caught Lucinda's eye. "Take the time to build the foundation before you blow the roof off the house." Wise words.

Lucinda had no desire to rush down a river that would later hit rapids and rocks, and Daniel felt the same way. Even with that agreement, they spent most of their free time together. Lucinda grew up on the mountain, and she showed him all of the places that echoed with her memories. She knew the best meadows and trails to find butterflies and the boulders to climb for the best views of the Tennessee River Gorge. She knew where to pick the best berries for jam.

As Daniel was getting to know Lucinda, he sometimes noticed a quiet sadness in her eyes. Something about this world had never lived up to her expectations, but maybe things were changing now. Along with the pure joy of dancing, a contra dance meant seeing Daniel, hearing his music, and dancing with him. Usually, he was on the stage with the band, but they reserved the first contra after the break and the final waltz at the end of the evening. She took the fabric remnants of her favorite dance skirts and sewed matching shirts for him to wear. Her latest creation was a "Star of the Bluegrass" twirly skirt, with the pattern continued on a shirt for Daniel. Lucinda still had disturbing dreams at times, but slowly and softly, her sadness dissolved the way fog melts under sunlight. As she came to know him and trust him, joy floated into her heart and her eyes. The sparkle she was born with returned to bless her mornings. She was so lit up with love that everyone could see it.

Lucinda invited Daniel to special exhibits at the Hunter Museum in Chattanooga, always with lunch at Rembrandt's, a café in the Bluff View Art District. The special on Saturday was tomato corn gumbo with okra, fresh baked bread, and a salad of local greens with goat cheese and heirloom tomatoes. At the museum, Lucinda liked to share ideas about what she saw – the way the artists used color and light, what made a particular painting or sculpture worthy of a museum, and what surprised her. That afternoon, the museum featured a new exhibit of mermaid paintings and sculptures, some traditional and some futuristic. Lucinda was especially taken with an abstract painting of a mermaid. Daniel asked her to share what she was seeing.

Lucinda studied the painting, then looked at Daniel. "Notice the way the coral is weaving pastel colors, shapes engaging each other, almost like dancers. The water merges into shades of aqua, pink and lavender. But the most amazing thing is the way the painter gives us transparency and light underwater. It's almost as though the mermaid's skin is transparent."

As he stood there with her, Daniel felt music coming to

him from the mysterious place. He opened his backpack, took out his pad of music paper, sat on a bench in front of the painting, and started writing the notes he was hearing. When he noticed Lucinda watching him, he told her, "I feel music coming from her skin." He took a few more minutes to finish the tune, which seemed to arrive by itself.

"What kind of tune is it?"

"A waltz. I'll play it for you, maybe tomorrow night. I'd like to keep it inside a while longer to see if another countermelody comes to me and work the harmonies."

Lucinda smiled. "And what about the statue over here?"

"It's a thirty-two bar reel in D minor. A great tune for clogging at the Mountain Opry. I'll keep it in mind before I fall asleep tonight and see what I dream."

"And this painting?"

"I'm hearing a serenade in G with music for mermaids. Water ballet. This one is ethereal, not a dance tune."

Lucinda had studied art at the University of Tennessee, Chattanooga, with a major in painting. Her family owned a goat farm with a large vegetable garden on Signal Mountain. They always had good food to eat but not a lot of money for tuition. On the basis of talent and need, she was given a full scholarship. Even as a student, she began to exhibit her work at galleries in Chattanooga, which helped provide money for art supplies. After she graduated, she returned to the farm but continued painting. Daniel was always eager to hear her observations, on a hike, at a dance or in a gallery. Since he experienced the world more through sound, her way of seeing opened his vision.

Later that afternoon, they walked to the River Gallery

on a corner close to the museum. Lucinda had exhibited watercolor paintings and quilts in several galleries in the Bluff View Art District. That spring, the River Gallery featured a group of her paintings, a series of Appalachian butterflies hovering around branches of a catalpa tree, painted in a wash of watercolors on handmade paper. Two of them had sold and four were still available. Daniel was quite taken with these paintings, one in particular, and wanted to buy it and take it home.

Lucinda said, "It's yours, but let's leave it here until after the show. I'll tell the gallery manager to mark it sold. And for you, the price is an original tune, preferably a waltz for mermaids."

The River Gallery felt like a folk museum for the local art culture, with paintings by local artists, sculpture in various media, ceramics, fabric art and jewelry. The rooms were full of pleasure for the eyes – a table of dolls made by artists from Signal Mountain, a case of lapis lazuli earrings and necklaces, a wall of paintings of dogwood trees, bridges over the Tennessee River, a raft with two children on Chickamauga Creek. Another room featured an artist who layered colors in a way that made you feel embraced by the sunset. As they wandered through the rooms of the early 20th century building that housed the gallery, they kept discovering new painters and photographers. In an earlier life, the building had been home to a large family.

At Lucinda's suggestion, they took a walk through the Sculpture Garden overlooking the Tennessee River. A cloud washed over Lucinda's face, perhaps a moment of memory. A pattern of leaves shadowed her face and hesitated before a return to sunlight.

When Daniel asked her about it, she told him, "I still have trouble trusting people. It's a long story, and I don't need to burden you."

"Believe me, I understand, even without the details. Not long ago, I didn't care if I ever saw a woman again."

"Before I met you, I was done with men. When my other friends got married, I went home to live with my Grandma. She was better company and we still have a wonderful time together."

"My best company was music for many years. It's why I've lived alone. But Lucinda, I hope you're starting to know you can trust me."

She hesitated.

"And if we get any closer, I won't ever want you to leave." He gathered her into a long, slow hug.

Something inside her relaxed in that moment. A cardinal flew to the shoulder of a sculpture of a mermaid, then to a low hanging branch close to her hand. It felt like an omen.

Chapter 4:

An Old Dream and a Promise

$\mathcal{F}$rom the time she was very young, Lucinda loved watching birds. She loved their music, loved watching them fly, and loved learning their names by the feathers. She filled the feeders by her windows with seeds and sugar water for the hummingbirds. Sometimes, she dreamed she was a bird, and if she was lucky when walking in the forest, she found a magic feather.

Lucinda loved to sing, especially in the forest as she walked the mountain trails. Her voice was high and clear, like a rainbow of light pouring through a stained glass window. For years, her time in the forest had been her place of solitude, embraced by trees. Now, Daniel joined her, with a fiddle or a banjo in his backpack. They carried fresh baked bread, cheese and tomatoes for a picnic, and on the boulders after lunch, Daniel improvised on the banjo or played fiddle tunes. The mountains were full of music from the birds, the wind, and the fiddlers who played the music Daniel had loved since he was very young. As they hiked on Signal Mountain, the mountain told them stories.

On Friday nights, Lucinda joined Daniel and his students at the Mountain Opry. What surprised them most was how easy it was to be together. The deep comfort they felt in each other's presence was something neither of them had felt before. After his students arrived with their banjos and fiddles, Lucinda put a rainbow of shawls on their chairs when they went backstage to warm up. Grandma often joined them and sat with her, as they had been doing for many years.

Weather permitting, weekends were for hiking. They watched the light change as the sun crossed the sky, revealing new faces of the mountain. The Appalachian Mountains, although millions of years old, always unveiled something new – a new species of butterfly, an exotic wildflower, ginkgo leaves with shadows like a pattern on a Persian tapestry. Lucinda liked to sit on boulders with a sketchbook and a charcoal pencil. Some of her images were realistic and other times, the lines of her drawings transformed what she saw. As she drew, Daniel tuned into the spirit of the mountain.

They watched the seasons change for a year with their love still blooming. One night, after an early dinner, he asked Lucinda to go with him on an evening hike to watch the moonrise. He had carefully chosen the place – their favorite lookout over the Tennessee River Gorge – and had waited for the evening of the full moon. Just before sunset, he asked Lucinda to marry him, the sky layered with shimmering stripes of color.

Lucinda froze. Daniel watched her take a deep dive inside herself. A flock of starlings flew overhead. They circled and flew to the branches of a sweetgum tree. Daniel put his hand in his pocket, his fingers circling his Grandma's engagement ring. He heard his Grandma whispering and felt her smiling. He looked at the radiant beauty of Lucinda's face.

Lucinda was struggling to speak, but in this moment, even a single word was difficult. The moon was beginning to rise over the river. An owl called in the distance. Finally, slowly, Lucinda said, "As much as I love you, I just can't do it."

"No?" He knew she was the right person and it felt like the right time.

"I'm so sorry, but I can't."

"This doesn't make sense to me. I love you, and from everything I've seen, you love me too."

It was hard for her to speak, but slowly she found her words. "I love you deeply." Again, she was silent, then spoke again. "I'm just not sure if marriage is the right path for someone as deeply committed to art as I am."

"Lucinda, this doesn't match what I feel from deep inside."

"I confuse myself sometimes."

"Let's keep walking and you can tell me why you feel this way." He took her hand. "I'm listening."

Lucinda was silent for a while but then began to speak. "When I was twelve years old, I decided I would never get married."

"That's unusual. Most girls that age dream about their wedding."

"I never was like that. I lived with my grandparents when I was growing up and we didn't go to any weddings. I only lived with my parents for a few years, and it's hard to remember them. I don't remember my father, but I have a photograph of my mother Grandma gave me and a few sweet memories. My mother died while trying to give birth to the baby who would have been my little sister. Bled to death. By the time they got her to the hospital in Chattanooga, it was too late. My father brought me to Grandma's house and went back to his people on the other side of the mountain. I never saw him again.

"I have dreams about my mother sometimes. They are sweet dreams. She holds me in her arms and sings to me."

"Do you dream about your father?"

"Sometimes I have nightmares about a man shoveling coal under the house." A shiver went up her spine.

"I asked my Grandma so many times to tell me about my father. She would always say, 'when you're older' or 'maybe later.' Finally, when I was twelve years old, she decided it was time to tell me what she knew. From what I heard about my father that afternoon, I decided he was a person I would never want to know. I can still hear Grandma's voice, saying, *I never felt right about him, but it was her choice. I gave both of them my blessing at their wedding. After your mother died, he set the house on fire. Almost burned half of the mountain.*"

"Oh my goodness!"

"Grandma said, 'Now you know and let's not talk about it again.'" That night, I decided I would never get married."

"Are you sure your Grandma did the right thing by telling you?"

"I wouldn't have left her alone until she did. I had to know. I already felt like he was a monster to leave me when I was four years old. That day, he became even more of a demon in my mind."

"Can I hug you?"

"I need a hug right now. I don't like thinking about him, and talking about him is even worse."

Daniel gave her a long, slow hug. He wanted to gather all of her sorrow in his arms and toss it to the wind. He also wanted to convince her that not all men act that way, but he knew it would take more time. Slowly, Daniel gathered his words. "I'm just so sorry to hear about all of this."

Lucinda looked at the moon and the way it lit Daniel's face.

Daniel felt the ring in his pocket, and from somewhere unseen, he felt his Grandma's presence. He remembered the fireflies on her farm, the way they lit the hills at night. He felt the warmth of the sweater she knit and gave him for Christmas when he was fourteen years old. From a deep place inside, he felt her wisdom and her love.

Daniel and Lucinda continued walking in moonlit silence. An hour later, they walked back to her house. On her porch by the front door, he wasn't quite ready for her to go inside. His words came slowly. "I've been thinking about everything you told me tonight. I can understand why you feel this way. But in all the years since that time, haven't you ever been tempted to reconsider? You made that decision when you were twelve years old. You're twenty-seven now."

"I don't know why I'm saying no. I don't feel good

about saying no, but somewhere inside – and I don't understand it right now – I feel paralyzed."

"Believe me, I've felt that way too at times. But Lucinda, we can have a much better life than they had. I'm a man of my word, and my word is gold. I will never leave you."

"I feel your love inside the atoms of every cell in my body, but the whole idea of marriage terrifies me."

"I don't need an answer now. Just think about it. Take your time but promise me you'll think about it."

"Okay . . . I'll think about it."

"That's all I need from you right now."

Chapter 5:

Seven Dreams

*D*aniel asked Lucinda to marry him seven times, in seven different places. The second time he asked, Lucinda got very quiet.

Daniel watched her face and asked, "Do you love me?"

She beamed a radiant smile. "Of course I do!"

"Then . . .?"

"Marriage is a different animal. I don't remember my father, and my Grandpa was a very quiet man. A good man, but I can't say I really knew him. I don't know how to live with a man."

"We can figure it out."

"I need time to think about it – maybe a lot of time."

Daniel was silent for a while. He took out his banjo and played Lucinda a traditional tune, something he learned years ago from the old time fiddlers. Then he played music that came to him in a dream. His Grandma was singing to him in that dream and he felt quietly confident. When he took Lucinda home that night, he hugged her at the door. A long and tender hug, then a kiss.

Before she went inside, he told her, "Take your time, honey. I know you're the right one. And now, sweet dreams."

In the morning after breakfast, Lucinda told her Grandma that Daniel wanted to marry her. Grandma smiled but said nothing. They sat together on the porch, stitching a quilt. Too much silence, so Lucinda asked what she was thinking. Grandma knew what everyone in the dance community knew but didn't believe in giving advice. She replied, "Daniel is a good man, but this is your life, not mine. You need to decide for yourself."

A few months later, after a barn dance, Daniel asked again. A fourth time while they were hiking, looking for berries. A year later, in the sculpture garden of the art museum. It was almost like a running joke between them. Each time, he had a new tune to play on the banjo or his violin.

They got to the point where they could talk about it calmly. Lucinda would tell him about her dreams and Daniel would share his vision. Every so often, he'd open the conversation again. "I can feel my future from a place so deep inside me. Doesn't it feel right to you?"

"It does feel right to be with you, but . . ."

"I've seen love that wasn't true before. This is the real thing."

"I know it doesn't have anything to do with you, but something inside me is still afraid."

"It takes time to get over a trauma like that, but I'm

confident you can do it. What scared you happened a long time ago. You're older now and you know a lot more about the world. Listen deep inside, and you might hear something different."

A few weeks later on a Friday night, he hid four dozen roses in the back of his truck and then drove to Lucinda's house for an early dinner before the barn dance. Other than the dangling marriage proposal, nothing had changed between them. During the first half of the dance, he played with the Half Moon Strutters. At the break, he sat with Lucinda for soup and cornbread, then did the first two dances with her. At the end of the dance, he played the first waltz with his band. For the second waltz, he walked off the stage to dance with Lucinda. Watching them move together was like ballet. Body to body in perfect harmony. A dip, a pivot, a lean toward the music. A twirl, an innuendo. A secret language only the two of them knew.

After the dance, he asked her, "What did you dream last night? I had the most amazing dream, and all day I have been wondering if you had it too. I woke up with music, a waltz, but I'm not quite ready to play it for you. I need to do something more unusual with the chords."

"Let me know when your tune is ready. I'm eager to hear it."

"And your dream?"

"The coal man again, but the dream dissolved into roses. Thousands of petals gently falling against my face, like a shower of falling stars, except it was roses. I was standing on a tropical island by the ocean, watching the sky. I walked into the water. It was turquoise, warm and salty, and I saw a mermaid! We swam together by a high cliff. It was a long time ago, an ocean I've never seen."

"Beautiful! I think you'll like the waltz I wrote for you. Something about the music I heard feels like a mermaid's dream."

When Daniel drove Lucinda home, he asked her to stay in the truck for a few minutes and close her eyes. With the roses from the back of the truck, he made a labyrinth of rose petals in her front yard. He placed votive candles in each of the four directions, with two candles and six roses in the center. After he lit the candles, he took Lucinda's hand and led her to the labyrinth.

When Lucinda opened her eyes, what she saw was mysterious and beautiful. Daniel held her hand and showed her where to enter. He followed her through the labyrinth, weaving the path slowly. In the distance they heard the call of an owl. All around them, moonlight shining through the trees. Daniel had his Grandma's engagement ring in his pocket, an antique beauty, and asked in silence, only with his eyes.

He knew she would say yes. His Grandma had appeared in a dream to give them her blessing, and he heard it in the wedding waltz he was writing. Now, he felt the whisper of his Grandma's promise. He took the ring out of his pocket, kissed Lucinda's hand, and gave her the ring.

She held it up to the moonlight to take a better look. "Oh, this is beautiful!"

"This was the ring my Grandma wore."

"What an honor."

"I can feel her blessing us right now."

"I feel it too."

Daniel watched as she slipped the ring onto her finger. He kissed her, and they hugged each other for a long time. A long slow hug that would ripple through the years.

They fell asleep on the porch swing with Lucinda leaning on his shoulder. Quilts and pillows all around them. In a dream, Lucinda watched the moon rise over the river. The moon continued to rise, then bloomed like a wildflower over the mountain. The dream would become a painting. Daniel heard mermaids singing in the echo of his waltz, with a light percussive rippling of the leaves. Lucinda heard it too. It felt like the mountain held them in its song.

Chapter 6:
Wedding in the Dance Barn

*L*ucinda and Daniel wrote their own ceremony, with some traditional elements, a sacred circle of poems, and their own vows. Grandma made Lucinda's wedding dress in silk and lace, and sewed a purple vest for Daniel. She made him a white silk wedding shirt in the style of nineteenth century vintage patterns. She had consulted the *Farmer's Almanac* and suggested a sunny day toward the end of May. Their wedding invitations were written in calligraphy with a watercolor painting of the dance barn, the violin on the silo, and 32 bars of music surrounding everything – the waltz Daniel wrote for Lucinda the night he met her. Lucinda invited her artist friends from Chattanooga. Daniel invited his students, and they both invited friends, musicians and dancers from the contra dance community.

The morning of the wedding, Lucinda's Grandma baked a carrot cake decorated with whipped cream, berries and wildflowers. Everyone met at the dance barn early in the afternoon. Daniel's students played Irish fiddle tunes as the guests arrived. As the bride and groom arrived in a horse-drawn carriage, the guests formed a large circle, holding hands. The ceremony began with a Scottish strathspey as the wedding party weaved a Spiral Dance to the center of the circle. Four dancers stepped into the circle to create sacred space with poems in the four directions. Then, an ensemble of Daniel's students stepped into the circle to play music he had composed for the ceremony, with fiddles, banjos, clarinet, cello, and bass. Grandma presided over the rest of the ceremony with the Justice of the Peace, as Lucinda and Daniel spoke their wedding vows. After the "I do's" and the exchange of rings, Grandma looked at Daniel and said, "You may now kiss your bride." He kissed her, twirled her and dipped her almost to the ground, then back up into a pivot bear hug – amid a full circle of whoops, hollers and applause.

The wedding feast followed with contributions from every wedding guest. They covered two long tables with salads picked from their gardens that morning, tomato corn chowder with okra, vegetables with a Japanese dipping sauce, fresh baked bread, two pots of chili with cornbread, churned butter and goat cheese, catfish from the river, sliced peaches and berries. Everyone brought their favorite treats in picnic baskets.

The Half Moon Strutters played for the wedding dance, combining traditional fiddle tunes with their own music. They began with a new waltz for Daniel and Lucinda – a beautiful melody with Daniel's signature of unexpected chords. The newlyweds had the telepathy that dancing lovers share, and nobody knew their dance was improvised. The way he looked at her, the way she smiled and glowed, it was clear to everyone how much they loved each other. With the second waltz, the wedding guests took partners and joined in the dancing. The dance continued with two contras before cutting the wedding cake. After a few toasts, the dance continued for another set and two more waltzes. By then, the horse-drawn carriage was back and waiting to carry the newlyweds into the sunset.

For their honeymoon, Daniel and Lucinda canoed along the snake of the Tennessee River and hiked on the Cumberland Trail. In the evenings, their passion discovered a deeper way of singing, a new kind of music. Her hands kneaded the mountains, rivers and trails of his muscles. He honored her with his loving every night, and their dreams wove together inside a divine tenderness. Above them, moonlight trickled through the trees, and owls called messages through their dreams. Lucinda took out her sketchbook in the morning to draw the images of her dreams in charcoal pencils, with poems and messages rippling through the trees. She filled a notebook with drawings of Daniel as he was composing music, or listening to the river, or hiking on the mountain. She also sketched the two of them in their canoe.

Sometimes music revealed itself while they were sleeping, and Daniel wrote what he heard in his notebook in the morning. Lucinda gave him a sanctuary of silence during these times, so the music would continue to reveal itself, along with chords and harmony. Later, a breakfast of mountain mint tea, granola, nuts and dried apricots. Time felt endless, even though time is an illusion, a bird flying through the forest as its blue wings disappear behind a tangle of trees.

Chapter 7:

The Soft Scent of Morning

*A*fter their honeymoon, Daniel and Lucinda found a historic house halfway up the mountain. It was more than a century old, with a porch that wrapped around the front and side of the building, and gardens surrounded by old growth trees. The Mountain People feel that every house has a soul, and the house chooses the people who live there. This house seemed to be calling for an artist and a musician, with an enclosed porch that could be used as an art studio, a large den for the music room, a living room with a fireplace, three bedrooms with a bird's nest view of the trees, and a kitchen that reminded Lucinda of her Grandma's house. They had to replace some wood that had been damaged by snow melt, along with the porch railing, but most of the house was structurally sound. The previous owners had already replaced the roof, and they had planted beautiful gardens with daffodils, tulips, tiger lilies, irises, columbines, heirloom roses, coneflowers and dogwood trees.

Daniel hired a musician friend who did plumbing and carpentry to replace the old iron pipes with copper. Sam drove up on his Harley. His shirt, sleeves cut at the shoulders, revealed his muscles and tattoos. The next morning, he came early in his father's pickup and brought a crew of two young men, his neighbors on the mountain, and the three of them got the job done in less than a week. Daniel replaced the window on the front door with stained glass, and then they were ready to move in, ten days before the start of the school year. Friends from the dance community helped them move their furniture up the mountain. Grandma, who was sewing curtains, cooked chili and baked cornbread muffins for everyone who helped.

After they moved in, Lucinda decorated the walls with watercolor paintings and quilts. She loved the way light filtered into the house, both sun and moonlight. Windows all around to enjoy the old growth trees, the gardens, and phases of the moon. Large windows in the music room and the kitchen to feel the sunlight, the intensity of thunderstorms, and the soft weight of snowfall in the winter. They were far enough away from city lights to observe the constellations, the milky way and meteor showers. The yard had a clearing surrounded by chinkapin oaks, loblolly pines and sweetgum trees, where squirrels and birds built their nests. In the spring, they constructed a greenhouse with hand-rolled glass, to start the seeds early and to continue growing food after the season turned colder. Even their early winter soups came from the garden.

Daniel continued teaching music in the local schools, with Friday nights at the Mountain Opry. Lucinda spent her days painting, inspired by her dreams, the birds who came to their feeders, and hikes on the mountain. She made skirts and dresses for a boutique in Chattanooga, colorful threads to swirl and dance. At barn dances around the state, "Lucinda skirts" were well known and admired for their swirls of color – an extra flourish for dancers who loved to spin, dip and twirl. Grandma knit socks to match the dresses, using yarn that was as soft as it was colorful. They used fabric remnants to sew quilts with traditional patterns and designs, along with new designs based on animals, dolphins, flowers, trees and birds. New shapes revealed themselves in her dreams, a kaleidoscope of color, and her quilts were featured at local galleries.

The quilt on their bed was the gift Daniel gave Lucinda on their wedding night – the quilt he had treasured for years with the whisper of his Grandma's promise. He felt her blessing in the patterns of turquoise, fuchsia and forest green, and in the interweaving fabrics of butterflies, leaves and flowers. Grandma had always chosen fabrics to echo the beauty in the world. Daniel loved his wife with his hands, his heart and his spirit. She was the mountain river where music flowed into his heart, sunlight on leaves in the early morning.

He wondered sometimes if all of this was a gift he had been given after struggling for centuries. He had read Hindu and Buddhist philosophy about how it takes many lifetimes to work through the lessons this planet gives and what we need to learn to free ourselves from the wheel of rebirth. He had seen other couples struggle and fight over petty things. Maybe it was because they had to wait so long to meet each other, but their way was to lean into the joy. Sometimes they had to talk about different ways they saw things, but it was an exploration, never an argument. They'd play out various angles of the situation until they found the way to harmonize the notes. Easy to do when you're playing in the same key.

As the season changed, snow fell and made the world quiet. Nights for music, warm soup, butter and bread. Frost on the windows like a pattern for a quilt. Spring came with the robins, and then a profusion of birds flying to the feeders. Their songs and the colors of their wings and bellies came flying through the yard and swirling in her skirts. Daniel and Lucinda planted first in the greenhouse and later in the yard. Herbs and vegetables for salads, stir fry dinners and soups. Berries for jam and artisan bread. Arbors of wisteria and grapes created mysterious tunnels of scent and taste – branches dripping and twisting like a mountain melody. In their garden, tiger lilies, coneflowers, columbines, irises and heirloom roses stretched toward the sun. Beautiful colors for the eyes, the tables, the windows, and the nightstand by their bed. Daniel chose them by the scent. Surrounded by flowers every night, he inhaled the scent of her skin. A scent that continued through the soft brush of morning.

Chapter 8:
Daniel's Dream

*H*uman creatures, like mermaids, are part animal and part angel. The animal wants to reproduce itself and continue singing. The angel wants to share her wisdom, intuition and art. The mermaid wants to whisper the ancient mysteries, a vision of sea cliffs and jagged rocks, filtered light rippling with the tide, light swimming inside currents of warm blue water. It's the kind of light that brings dreams with messages to people above the water, but to only those who listen to the music of their souls.

Daniel's dream appeared just before sunrise, like an earthquake rippling across the mountains. He saw himself alone, playing the banjo in a cabin by the ocean, high on a rocky coast. A cove below, a steep drop from the cliffs. Something mysterious, like a mermaid, underwater. The dream disturbed him, but it disappeared inside the light of morning.

Jolted awake, he reached for his wife and held her close. She sighed from the hidden cave of a dream but didn't wake up. Not until the light hit her eyes through the branches of a catalpa tree. A hummingbird drank sugar water by the window, darted higher up the mountain. The music in his dream made him shiver. He cradled his wife in his arms, pulled her closer and whispered, "Don't ever leave me."

That morning, their love-making reached into the place between the worlds, the water where new souls come into being. DNA swam, met and formed a new union in tunnels filled with starlight. A wish and a promise, a mermaid's dream, ancient and new as the sunlight in the morning.

Lucinda knew immediately. She leaned against her pillow and said, "Daniel, did you feel what I just felt? A new life is shining inside me. I feel her spirit in my body." This was confirmed two weeks later. Full moon, no blood.

Chapter 9:
The Little Swimmer

*I*t was mysterious the way her body changed during those nine months. Sometimes Lucinda was full of energy and sometimes she needed to rest, but it was amazing to know that a baby was growing inside her. During the seventh week, while she was starting to paint one afternoon, she sensed a tiny heart beating. It filled her with wonder. She sat on a boulder beside a rhododendron tree and listened to everything around her. Then she followed her feelings with a pencil and a brush. Branches of the tulip tree stretching out to flowers, early spring, with the light fading to early evening. Fireflies and fairies all around.

Every morning, before he drove down the mountain to teach, Daniel brought her a cup of ginger tea and a slice of toast with jam. Strawberry or apricot. It helped with the morning sickness. Later in the day, Lucinda enjoyed making soup and baking – artisan breads swirled with cheese and herbs, cinnamon rolls with dried fruit, and gingerbread cookies. But certain foods she couldn't eat and didn't want to smell. For nine months, no onions in the soup.

Lucinda felt the soul inside her, cells multiplying, becoming skin, bones and blood. Tiny organs forming. Fingers, hands and feet. She asked the new soul, "Do you have a name?"

The name she heard was *Arianna*.

When he returned from teaching, Daniel hugged his wife and put his ear next to her belly. Every day, he longed to hear the tiny heartbeat. It filled him with awe. As he sat by the fireplace with his arms around Lucinda, songs would come in phrases that kept singing through the night. He heard the music first on the banjo, with rhythms on the bass. Later, he improvised a countermelody on the violin.

Sometime between the fourth and fifth month, Arianna started moving and kicking. At first, it felt like a butterfly wing – something fluttering inside. Then stronger. In the evening, Daniel liked to take out his banjo or a wooden flute and play music for mother and child, feeling the magic of a new soul growing. Sometimes he'd play a fiddle tune as a lullaby.

Lucinda painted through her pregnancy. The birds that came to the feeder by her window, the trees that grew on Signal Mountain, and the way light changed through the seasons. She was inspired by the flowers in her garden and the wildflowers on trails up the mountain. One night, she saw a rainbow in the clouds at sunset. Later, moonlight filled their yard. In the morning, she painted Daniel in a wash of watercolors, outside on a boulder in their yard, playing banjo. Then a charcoal pencil to heighten the fine lines of his muscles and the shadows.

She knew her cravings were what her daughter would want to eat as she grew. Ginger tea, strawberries and blueberries, potato dill bread, melons, cucumbers, tomatoes and goat cheese. As her belly was forming stretch marks, she continued to be amazed by the miracle of it all. Her breasts became heavier, preparing to fill with milk. The air became thick with summer.

Every night before they feel asleep, Daniel loved listening to Arianna's tiny heartbeat. Mysterious music. The rhythm of life.

"Two hearts beating inside me now."

"Both beautiful!"

Daniel moved closer, under their summer quilt. "When I put my hands on your belly, I can feel her moving."

"But sometimes she likes to wake up and dance, right when I lie down exhausted and need to sleep!"

The ninth month of pregnancy was not comfortable. Sometimes at night, Lucinda felt like the entire universe was moving and stretching within her belly. She was excited, exhausted, elated. She felt the baby's head drop low into her pelvis and said to Daniel, "The baby has outgrown the tiny apartment and needs more living space."

Daniel, like most fathers, felt a bit helpless. He tried to reassure her. "Just a few more weeks."

"I'm really getting tired of waking up ten times a night, and my back aches right now."

"Let me give you another back rub."

That always helped, also massaging her feet and hands. But then the little swimmer would kick again, rippling waves across her belly.

"She is playing marimba on my ribs and drums on my bladder. It's crazy and sublime."

"This is giving me ideas for my second grade marimba and xylophone class. You should hear those kids! Such a joyful noise! A magical riff of sounds!"

"Just be glad you don't have to sleep with the marimba choir in your belly!"

Even with the discomfort she felt, Lucinda did not forget about the miracle. It was a kind of instinctual knowing – a rarefied space, tingling with silence. She was always aware that a whole person was swimming inside her belly, and it felt natural to talk to her all day. Often, she had strong feelings she knew were coming from the baby.

Sometimes, while she was sleeping under the soft light of autumn stars, Lucinda saw visions. Sometimes angels and fairies, and a cello from somewhere unseen, playing mysterious music. A dolphin swimming in a sunrise of amethyst light, swimming with mermaids. The shadow of a young girl rippling through green water. A water lily, a forest of seaweed dancing. Lucinda's nights swelled with wisdom dreams, and waking up so many times each night helped her remember them. She had a sketchbook by her bed and painted her visions in the morning.

In a parallel universe, grandmothers whispered secrets. Lucinda heard their singing in the voices of the leaves, the low tones of the trees, and the hum of the mountain. Her style of painting changed – a woman becoming a tree, mythical birds with jewels on their wings. Light becoming prisms of color, a dance, an awakening. Somehow, she felt her daughter would bring music into the world. In November the Leonid meteor showers fell for three nights, and later they lit up her paintings. A moon, a stripe of light over the river, a path of silver.

In dreams, her husband played the lyre for her, a touch, a sliding that rippled through her body. Sometimes a violin, sometimes a banjo rippling like a river. When they entered the holy fire in the shrine of her sacred roses, the world lit up with their singing.

Chapter 10:

Birth on the Mountain

*A*rianna continued to dream inside the half moon of her mother's belly. At night, she swam with dolphins in currents of tropical water. They carried her to shore. Lucinda's waters broke at sunrise. Mermaids had been swimming in her sleep all night. They anointed her with salt and she swam with them. The contractions began gently, then started to build in their intensity.

Daniel held his wife and massaged her back. He brought her a cup of honey ginger tea and called the midwife, a dancer with healing hands. Waves of contractions rippled through Lucinda's body. This she endured, breathing through the pain. Deep inside her, she felt the contractions vibrate, become intense and then back off. Like a wave coming and crashing. Then another wave. And another wave.

When it felt like more than she could bear, the midwife

put her in the shower. Warm water flowing gave her respite from the labor pains. She wanted to stay in the water, to give birth there. Naked in the shower, she sat on the birthing stool. The maple tree from which it was carved held her in its arms. Water on her belly and her back, soothing the labor pains. Then she moved back to the birthing bed.

A birth is a gift of love, a miracle, an altered state of consciousness. A river of joy running through a river of pain. Daniel breathed with her, in joy and amazement. Despite an intensity of pain she had never before known, Lucinda's eagerness to see her child kept whispering music of the miracle. Daniel brought soup for the midwife when he sensed she needed nourishment. He massaged Lucinda's back and her hands to help ease the pain.

The waves of birth kept coming, more and more powerfully now. In silence, Daniel massaged her hands and her shoulders. He held her in his loving gaze. The intensity built until it felt like more than she could endure, followed by an uncontrollable urge to push. Two pushes for the head. One for the shoulders. Two more for the tiny hips.

In the early afternoon, as her dreams had predicted, a baby girl was born. Floating into the world in a wave of rushing water. After the midwife caught her, Arianna cried to clear her lungs. She was so beautiful, mysterious eyes full of the other world and seeing this one for the first time. The midwife placed her on Lucinda's chest, and Arianna's tiny mouth found her mother's breast, now swelling with milk.

In that moment, the three of them fell mercilessly in love. A bigger love than anyone could have imagined.

Despite the pain, Lucinda knew she would do it all over again, just for that first newborn gaze. Soon, exhaustion swept over her, and the three of them fell asleep. Dreams of dolphins. Dreams of mermaids. Dreams of rushing water.

Chapter 11:

Banjos, Butterflies and Bach

*I*n those early weeks, the world was still warm. Humidity rose from the river, and the air was full of butterflies. Birds came to the feeder every morning – their colors and songs brought joy. Lucinda liked to sit by the trees to nurse. Sometimes next to a maple, sometimes by the rhododendron, sometimes under the branches of a catalpa tree. She liked to watch the shadows of their heart shaped leaves, with changing patterns of sunlight on the ground.

Lucinda's style of painting and drawing changed after the birth of her daughter. With charcoals, she drew her daughter in a sketchbook – a new drawing almost every day. When Arianna started to crawl, she often had to work quickly. She took her baby into the yard and watched her exploring everything she saw. Arianna with flowers, birds, a baby bunny, the neighbor's calico cat, a dragonfly. She began to add fairies to her paintings. Watercolors of wildflowers with fairies in a meadow. A fairy picnic on the roots of a catalpa, with wild berries and tiny cups of tea. A fairy on Arianna's outstretched hand.

Daniel played music every night for his daughter and his wife. Sometimes on the fiddle, sometimes on a wooden flute or a banjo. Music was always the way Arianna slipped from waking into a dream. Lucinda and her Grandma made a quilt for Arianna's wall with dolphins, tropical fish, and a mermaid. Grandma came often to play with the baby, bake bread and cook for the family. Arianna was her joy.

On the wall by Arianna's crib, Lucinda framed a painting of a mermaid, and over the chiffarobe, a profusion of butterflies. Sometimes, Arianna swam with mermaids in her dreams. She didn't yet have the language to tell anyone, but she knew the mermaid was her friend. For her daughter's first birthday, Lucinda framed two watercolor paintings for the wall by her window, each one a pastel celebration of wildflowers, a songbird, a butterfly and a fairy. Grandma baked the birthday cake.

Arianna loved to hear her father play the banjo. She ran to sit under the piano when he composed, and she loved the string bass. She liked being close to the sound and feeling the vibration of the notes in her body. She put her tiny hands on the back of the bass while he was playing to feel the notes in her fingers and told her father she wanted to play it with him. Her father lifted her up to the fingerboard and showed her how to pluck the strings. She needed her whole hand to do it. Then he said, "Arianna, it's too big for you. When you get older, I'll teach you how to play the cello. Come and see."

He took his cello out of the music cabinet, tuned it, and started playing. First, some long low notes so Arianna could feel the vibration. Then some scales and improvisation, to show her the range and timbre of the notes. Then Bach. Then, with her hand on his, he played open strings.

Often when the moon was full, shining through the branches of the sweetgum tree, Arianna would dream about the mermaid. She would visit an enchanted world underwater, swim with banded fish, and learn amazing things from the mermaid grandmothers. The mermaid promised they would meet one day, but in a different place and time. In the morning, Arianna came down to breakfast and told her parents, "I am the mermaid's sister."

Chapter 12:
The Swan

*W*henever her father played music, Arianna ran into the room. One afternoon, when Daniel was playing a fiddle tune on the piano, he walked away to get staff paper to write a few chords for his students. Arianna walked over to the piano and played the same tune. Daniel came back and played another part of the tune. He played it again and nodded to his daughter. Arianna listened and watched, then played it.

Lucinda was standing at the door, amazed by what she heard and saw. That was the moment she knew her daughter would be a musician. As Daniel was experimenting with chords under the melody, Lucinda opened a sketch book and began to draw her husband and daughter, now three years old, at the piano. Arianna played the tune again, and Lucinda asked, "How do you know how to do this?"

Without hesitation, Arianna told her, "I heard music before I was born. When I was playing with other children at the baby farm."

"The baby farm?"

"That's where babies wait to be born."

"Who took care of you at the baby farm?"

"Fairies and angels. You know, like the fairies in your paintings."

"And music?"

"We all love music! Sometimes, it sounds like birds. Other times, a humming or a song.

"What happens when you are born?"

"You slide down the Earth Tunnel."

Her father smiled and continued to teach her the tune, "Round the Horn." Two days later, he taught her another tune, "Star of the County Down." A week later, "*La Maison de Glace.*" He told her, "Music is a beautiful language. Keep listening."

Daniel began to teach her to play the piano, first by ear and then showing her which notes go with which keys. "This is A, this is B, this is C. Now close your eyes and tell me what I am playing."

Arianna was easy to teach because of her natural gift with music. When she was almost four years old, he gave her a very small cello. Her first lesson began with a bear hug around the cello. He showed her pizzicato on the open strings, and then asked her to play it on her cello. A few days later, he had her name the open strings he was playing with her eyes closed. Then he placed a small bow in her hand, showed her how to hold it and how to draw the bow across the strings. He began to teach her notes in the first position. First on the D string with tunes using those notes. Then on the A string, with a week for practice, adding a new string each week. This delighted her. The teaching method he used – he plays, she plays – what some of the music kids called "monkey see, monkey do." She'd get the sound in her ear and then match it.

Arianna loved the way the cello looked. *Beautiful wood*, she thought, *so curvy. I've never seen anything as beautiful.* Her hands were flexible and she had a really good ear.

Her father taught her to phrase her bowing with simple melodies – he'd sing a tune for her and then ask Arianna to sing it. Unlike some of his students who were too shy to sing, his daughter did not hesitate.

"Notice how the breath will only allow you to go so far before you have to take another breath?"

"You have to breathe or you'd run out of air."

"When you're singing, there are natural places to take a breath. Phrasing your bow strokes on the cello is the same way. That's where you end the phrase and change the direction of your bow."

"Like this?" She played the melody she was learning with attention to phrasing choices. Her father made a few suggestions, played the tune for her, and then she played it again. With better and better expression each time.

"A phrase is like a sentence, like breathing. You need to breathe and so does the music."

She took a deep breath and played the piece again, with even more expression.

For Arianna, music was a natural language. Whenever Daniel suggested something, she understood and changed the way she was playing. She moved easily through the first two Suzuki books. Later, when she learned to play "The Swan," she liked to imagine a beautiful swan floating peacefully through the water. Her beautiful cello was curved like a swan.

Daniel encouraged her to make up stories about the music she was playing. She also liked to give colors to the notes. *That's a blue note. This one is yellow. This tune is like the sun. This one is a river.* She loved to sit under the piano when her father was composing. What he didn't know is that while he was doing this, she was composing her own songs.

Later that year, Lucinda became pregnant again. A pregnancy will bring a woman inward, but she had a child to care for this time. So when she wanted quiet time in the yard, she brought Arianna with her. Mother and daughter painted together, gathered herbs, and drank star anise tea in the garden. They made bread with fruit, nuts and herbs from the garden, and they shared their dreams. As Lucinda's belly swelled, Arianna wanted to know all about how a baby grows. Daniel brought home a book from the library with beautiful pictures to illustrate the stages of growth for the nine months. He read it to his daughter as a bedtime story.

One night, Arianna brought her cello into her parents' bedroom to play music for the baby. "I want the baby to hear the music through your tummy." She played long, low notes, then she played "The Swan" for the baby who was floating. She improvised a tune and then put her ear on her mother's belly to listen for the baby's heartbeat.

At night, Lucinda left the curtains open for the moon

to shine on her belly and her bed. New life was again swimming inside her, a tiny miracle. One night, she dreamed about a mermaid coming to shore on an island far away, in another time. Maybe the distant past or the future. The mermaid swam to the beach where she was waiting. At sunrise, the beautiful mermaid with green eyes and flowing red hair brought her a necklace of pearls, then gazed into her eyes. It was a moment of recognition, as though they were two Egyptian priestesses meeting again after swimming through time. Then, without warning, she sang something in her high, beautiful voice, a song for the dolphins swimming in the cove. A fog drifted in as she dove under a blue wave and returned to ancient water.

In another dream, the mermaid showed her a vision – a boy playing the violin on a high cliff over the ocean. Just after the new moon, Lucinda gave birth to a boy. A home birth with a midwife and just a few hours this time. Jeremy was full of music as soon as he was born. From the first cry.

Chapter 13:

Jeremy and His Violin

*J*eremy was born with a craving for musical instruments, especially the violin. Every night, his mother sang him a lullaby and gave him a back rub. Then his father would play a fiddle tune and a waltz to help him fall asleep. On Friday nights, he went in the baby basket with his parents and his sister to the Mountain Opry. For a while, he'd sit up and listen to the music. Then, he'd fall asleep with music in his dreams.

Just as his father had done for him, Daniel gave his son a tiny violin as soon as he could hold a bow. In the beginning, Daniel played open strings on his violin, and Jeremy imitated him. Daniel told him the names of the strings. He'd name a note and play it. Then he asked his son to close his eyes and name the note he was playing. It was his favorite game to play with his Dad, who was building a strong foundation for playing in tune.

Like most Suzuki students, his first tune was "Twinkle, Twinkle, Little Star." He learned everything by ear, with a gradual shift to looking at the music, but only after he had the tune memorized. Daniel wanted him to be able to play by ear and improvise with folk musicians along with developing good classical technique, since many of the folk musicians and fiddlers in the Appalachian Mountains could not read music.

As he grew, this was his special time with his father, along with Friday nights at the Mountain Opry. By the time he was six years old, he delighted the older fiddlers with traditional tunes in the first set. Sometimes, Jeremy woke up with music and played it for his family in the kitchen. He asked his sister to play with him, and she improvised harmonies – something her father had taught her to do, working with the root of the chord and then arpeggios. She matched the rhythm of her brother's cadence and sometimes added a countermelody. They'd practice the new tune for a while, and if their father was home, they'd ask him to get the bass and play with them. Sometimes, the three of them played during an early set at the Mountain Opry. More often than not, a banjo player would walk up to the stage to play with them.

When Lucinda took her children to Chattanooga, Jeremy liked to play the violin at the bakery by the River Gallery. He walked from table to table giving serenades, and sometimes people put tips in his case. Arianna played her cello in the gallery by her mother's quilts. Lucinda made skirts for her that matched the quilts, and they were often photographed. People came over to listen to the music, and many quilt purchases began this way. Lucinda made a series of quilts with musical themes, and it was never long before someone at the gallery wanted to take one of them home. She researched patterns of sacred geometry from around the world and rendered them in fabric. She taught both of her children how to design quilts and how to patch them together. It was a good family activity for the winter, during the cold time of the year.

Lucinda braided her daughter's long red hair every morning and tied her braids with rainbows of ribbons. After a breakfast of oatmeal, lemon-mint tea, yogurt and fruit, Arianna went to school with her Dad, her brother, her books, her homework, and her cello.

Jeremy was not shy. He took his violin to school and played fiddle tunes with friends. He played in the school orchestra – any kind of music was his friend. His best friend's Dad played banjo and taught his son, so the boys played music together after school. After milk and cookies, they liked to make up tunes. Homework had to wait and at times did not get done. Jeremy sat by his father on Friday nights to jam with older musicians at the Mountain Opry, and everyone was charmed by this young boy who was full of music. He loved playing for an audience. He loved the sound of the notes. Whenever someone showed him a new tune, he began to play along and soon, he knew it. That was the way the old fiddlers shared their music with the next generation. Jeremy took his violin to the lookouts on Signal Mountain, playing fiddle tunes for anyone who came near. Sometimes the birds, sometimes a raccoon or a chipmunk, sometimes a couple of hikers who would stop and listen.

By the time Jeremy was eight years old, he knew he

would be a musician when he grew up. He couldn't live without music. He had given up his desire to be a fireman or an astronomer. Music was more important. He always had music inside him when he did anything – riding his bicycle, playing baseball, hiking, doing homework at night. He woke up with music in the morning.

Along with the improvisations they did together, Arianna played classical duets with him. Simple duets at first, and later, the Bach Two-Part Inventions arranged for violin and cello. Arianna also enjoyed playing them on the piano. Their Dad brought home a book of duets arranged from other pieces: Dvorak's *Humoresque*, a Brahms' *Hungarian Dance*, Massenet's *Meditation from Thais*, Tchaikovsky's theme from *Swan Lake*, waltzes from *Sleeping Beauty*, the Albinoni *Adagio*, and Handel's *Water Music*. As they grew in their musical ability, they played duets by Ravel, Kodály and Glière. Jeremy was always coming up with new tunes, and Arianna liked to improvise countermelodies. She loved the sound of something new coming from the river of music she always felt inside her.

Like other boys his age, Jeremy liked to catch fireflies and bring them into his bedroom at night. He liked to watch them sparkle into constellations, and he would always leave his window open so they could fly out while he was dreaming. Unlike other boys his age, he would never keep them in a jar.

Chapter 14:

Rafting on the Hiawassee River

*D*uring the summer vacation each year, Daniel liked to travel with his family. For the first few weeks of June, Lucinda helped her daughter design a quilt and sew skirts for the next year at school. Arianna was at the age where she was always growing. Jeremy went to a two week Suzuki music camp in Illinois. They all hiked on Signal Mountain, exploring the trails and lookouts. As they hiked, they listened to the music of the mountain, the music of the wind, and the music of the insects and the birds. That was how the children learned to name the birds by their feathers and their songs. Arianna noted each new species of butterfly and drew them in her sketchbook. She kept a set of colored pencils in her backpack, with enough shades to render the colors accurately. Lucinda also made sketches and later worked in watercolors, filling in details with a Rapidograph pen.

By the end of June, everyone in the family felt a restlessness to explore something farther away from home. They packed their camper with four sleeping bags, a kerosene lantern, a Coleman stove, two fiddles, a banjo, a cello, maps and an atlas. They filled the camper's cabinets with dried fruit and nuts, granola, split peas, red lentils, cheese, crackers, apples, oranges, potatoes, carrots, chocolate chip cookies, fig bars and a few other treats. They would find the rest of their food at farmers markets and roadside stands.

They traveled to places of natural beauty – the Red River Gorge in Kentucky to see the rock formations, sandstone arches and natural bridges. The trails were full of exotic butterflies, more species than they had ever seen before. Two days later, they drove to the Cumberland River Gorge to hike on the trails by Cumberland Falls. They were hoping for clear skies to see the Moonbow and timed their visit during the five day cycle of the full moon. Daniel, Arianna and Jeremy joined the musicians jam as everyone waited for the moon to rise. The night forest was full of fireflies, then an arc of rainbow light rising up from the waterfall. They continued their cross country odyssey to the Grand Canyon and hiked on the Bright Angel trail, amazed by the geological history etched into the cliffs. At the gift store, Arianna picked out a geode to take home, and Jeremy chose a slice of agate.

The next summer, they visited Smoky Mountain National Park, climbed Lookout Mountain, and had a picnic by Ruby Falls. They drove to Georgia to hike in Cloudland Canyon State Park, Chattahoochee National Forest and Mount Yonah. They rafted on the Hiawassee

River and caught fish for dinner at night. At a roadside stand by the river, they feasted on buttermilk biscuits, fried green tomatoes, corn on the cob, and sweet potato pie. After a few days of rafting, they found a diner that served breaded catfish, turnip greens, and sweet potato fries. Peaches and ice cream for dessert.

To explore their local history, they visited the Chickamauga Battlefield and the Chattanooga Choo-Choo. They read biographies of people who lived during the Civil War and tried to imagine what those times were like. Kentucky and Tennessee had people fighting on both sides – hard to imagine. In the mountains of Upper Eastern Tennessee, people did not have slaves and sided with the North. The next summer, they went to Atlanta, Savannah, Shiloh, Greenville, Gettysburg and Washington, D.C. At night, they read biographies of Abraham Lincoln and Robert E. Lee by kerosene light. Later in the month, they hiked on Roan Mountain, savoring the glorious rhododendrons.

During the school year, they would search for the next adventure. The Blue Ridge Mountains and Nantahala National Forest made the short list, along with a hike on the Fiery Gizzard Trail. On a hike along Georgia's Raven Cliff Falls Trail, they found sparkle rocks in the river. They were always looking for a new waterfall or a river with canoes for the afternoon. A handful of smooth stones from the river was always a treasure.

Jeremy made up songs about everything he saw. Family favorites were a song about a waterfall who loved to sing, a firefly who gave musical dreams to children at night, rafting on the Hiawassee River, Aladdin's Palace in the Mark Twain Cave, hiking on the Blue Ridge Mountain trails, and a black bear who lumbered through their campsite one night.

One morning Arianna told her Mom, "I would worry about the world if Jeremy ever stopped singing."

Chapter 15:

The Language of Music

*W*hen Arianna played the cello, music was her friend. The notes were hummingbirds flying in un-expected patterns and directions, weaving through time. Watching Arianna play, anyone could see that the music was coming from a deep place inside her. She shaped the notes, expanding and condensing her hand. She practiced a wide vibrato to add texture and color to the music. The beautiful mermaid who came to visit in her dreams shared the songs she learned from her grandmothers. They were haunting and ethereal. She didn't visit often, but when she did, the dreams brought visions, music and messages.

Arianna kept learning pieces that were more and more challenging. She played in the orchestra her father conducted and sometimes improvised her own music. She loved the resonance of the low notes but also loved the tone of higher octaves as she moved toward the bridge on the fingerboard. She learned to play scales in three octaves and later four. Arianna understood the language of music and devoted many hours to practice. If a piece or a part was difficult, she took it on as a challenge, determined to perfect each passage.

When her family went to hear the Chattanooga Symphony, she was especially drawn to the cellist who played in the first chair of the second stand. Janine Silver was tall and thin, with wavy chestnut hair held away from her face with a rhinestone barrette. She found ways to vary the concert classical black – a tiered skirt, a lace blouse, or a black silk punjabi. Arianna always wanted to sit where she could listen and watch her play. Janine had a joyful and relaxed way of playing, but at the same time, played with tremendous passion and power. Since Daniel's primary instrument was the violin, he took Arianna backstage to meet her favorite cellist and made arrangements for Arianna to take lessons from her.

Arianna was easy to teach. She liked to practice and had an innate musical sense. When Janine gave her suggestions, Arianna was able to understand what she wanted immediately and incorporate the new technique. She developed a natural vibrato in the same style as her beloved teacher. She adored the Bach Unaccompanied Cello Suites and what they expressed, musically and emotionally. There was so much to explore – fingerings, bowings, dynamics, where the phrases needed to sing and breathe. Janine showed her where the passages echoed each other, each with a different dynamic.

Every Tuesday after school, Daniel drove his daughter and her cello to Chattanooga. Janine kept the door open to her studio so he could listen. Sometimes after the lesson, Janine put apple cider and ginger cookies on the kitchen table and welcomed the extra time to talk about music. She shared with Daniel, "When I'm teaching Bach, often a student hasn't given much thought to what a phrase is. A musical phrase is always going somewhere, never static. When I explain it to Arianna – the way a phrase is like a sentence, and where the phrase breathes – she understands everything so easily that I almost feel she was born knowing it.

"When playing Bach, the entire movement has an innate structure. Everything is building to a climactic point; therefore, you have to hold back some energy before you get there. When I shared this with Arianna, her playing became even more musical. If it's all right with you, I'd like to prepare your daughter to audition for the Chattanooga Youth Orchestra."

Daniel looked at his daughter. "Arianna?"

Without hesitation, she joined the conversation. "Yes, I'd love that. Even the first time I heard them give a concert, I knew I wanted to play with them." Arianna's face lit up with a radiant smile.

When she auditioned for the Chattanooga Youth Orchestra, she played the Prelude from the Second Bach Cello Suite. It was clear to the conductor and the symphony musicians who had volunteered that day, that unlike many of the other students who were playing notes, Arianna was playing music. Her playing was expressive, her intonation was spot on, and she made the first chair. Two of her friends made the violin section, and one of the boys, who was very talented, made principal clarinet.

The first year, they rehearsed and performed Beethoven's *Egmont Overture*; "Habanera" and "Les Toreadors" from Bizet's *Carmen*; and "Spring" from Vivaldi's *Four Seasons*. The next concert included Rossini's *Overture to William Tell* and the first movement of Beethoven's Fifth Symphony, along with an orchestral suite by a local composer. A year later, Jeremy auditioned for the Youth Orchestra, made the cut, and played in the back of the first violin section. He rode the bus with his sister and her friends to Chattanooga. They played the *English Folk Song Suite* and *Fantasia on a Theme by Thomas Tallis* by Ralph Vaughn Williams for their next concert. In the spring, they performed Mozart's *Eine Kleine Nachtmusik*, excerpts from Rogers' *Victory at Sea*, and Beethoven's First Symphony. There was always something new to discover and enjoy.

Their conductor had a style that worked well with young musicians. He always seemed to know what the composer wanted, and he inspired his orchestra to play it that way. He had stories to help each section play with expression and emotion. "Play this passage like a cat walking through an attic." "Play this like sunshine is pouring into the room." "We want to give our audience goose bumps here." With dynamics, he was able to create large changes in expression in a short amount of rehearsal time.

For their winter holiday concert, the All City Chorus joined them for several selections, ranging from early music to contemporary. They also played Tchaikovsky's *Waltz of the Sugar Plum Fairy*, Leroy Anderson's *Bugler's Holiday* and *Sleigh Ride*. After a standing ovation, they played Anderson's *Plink, Plank, Plunk* for a splashy encore. Then the All City Chorus came back on stage for the Hallelujah Chorus from Handel's *Messiah*.

All of the young musicians were mentored by musicians from the Chattanooga Symphony. During sectionals, the mentors shared musical technique, tips on how to practice, and what it's like to be a professional musician. They knew that some of these young musicians would go to conservatory and one day play in professional symphony orchestras.

Chapter 16:
Mermaid Initiation

*W*hen the season changed, Lucinda had a long sequence of dreams about worlds she had not seen before. Sometimes from a different part of our planet, sometimes from a different place in time. Two or three times a week, visions revealed themselves in her sleep. Always after a night of loving. Her visions inspired a new wave of paintings in a different style, a wash of watercolors filled with holy water.

Some of the dreams were dark, and they made her worry about the planet. She saw rivers drying up and the world coming to an end. No water. Everything burning. Birds trying to fly with fire in their feathers. And then, the world going dark. She had to wake Daniel after these dreams so he could hold her. Both of them worried that her dreams might one day become true.

She couldn't fully understand what was going on inside her, so she began painting to discover what her visions would reveal. Her paintings became mythological, mysterious abstractions, journeys into new dimensions. The size of the canvas expanded – sometimes a single painting, sometimes a triptych. On a painting she called "Mermaid Initiation," she wrote these words over waves that lifted like birds, becoming calligraphy:

Hours of twilight,
then an electric sky
at the edge of salty water.

Fish scales, a trout swimming upriver, gills
where the animal meets the angel,
a silver line of fins.

She swims in an ocean phosphorescent
like her skin
after hours of loving.

Silver waves
shimmer with an inner light
as she remembers the trajectory

and the promise
of the shining ones,
whispered before the flood

before the fire, before the rain –
voices of swimming lanterns,
angels, dolphins, visions under water.

Arianna had her own visions. At breakfast one morning, she told her parents that a mermaid swam with her in her dreams – the same mermaid who visited her when she was very young. The mermaid had been watching her grow, and like Arianna, she had long, wavy red hair. She sang to Arianna in a high soprano voice and asked her to play the music of the waves on her cello. The music was celestial, fragile, pastel – from a world she couldn't remember in the morning. Or maybe from a distant star. The mermaid told her a secret, wisdom from an earlier time, something her grandmother told her, but her words disappeared into the soft light of morning.

Lucinda opened a sketchbook. She drew what she felt, without thinking. Maybe the lines of her drawing would help her daughter remember.

Chapter 17:

Just before Dawn

*T*he whole family began having unusual dreams, full of art and music. Jeremy was dreaming a violin concerto, with melodies, chords and cadenzas to write down in the morning. Arianna swam with her mermaid sister. One night, she took Arianna to the cave where the mermaid grandmothers held counsel. The prophesy stones revealed that they would meet in the future – in life, not just a dream. When and where they would not say. Daniel often woke up with fiddle tunes, as he had for years, but the harmonies were getting more complex. He wrote them down in the morning, clearly some of his best work.

Lucinda's dreams inspired another new wave of paintings. Often, they arrived as visual poems. As she crossed the bridge at dawn, Lucinda walked over time, carrying a basket of pears in the early morning light.

Brushes and paint, the sun and the moon swirling out of expectations and form, orbits of color searching for a new shape.

Earlier in her life, art was a simple rendering – the striated layers of sunset, the arc of a willow branch, a deer running through a field of coneflowers. But the shapes lost the ability to hold themselves. They became stars, meteors, a supernova of color at the moment a star collapses. Light, brush strokes and form, the devotion of lovers curled around each other, finding a new shape every morning.

It was a time in her life when shapes began to sing, and she could hear their interweaving melodies, pastel skies and hues of melon splashing over her canvas. Life was what she saw, walking across fields of sunflowers in a warm summer wind, roses blooming by the side of the road, every petal having its own dream.

The petals filled the sky like meteor showers, arcing across midnight when she walked in the moonlight, tossing time through a prism of light. The world was what she saw and would never see again – a painting of her husband in the early morning; a river littered with tiny stones of agate, jade and jasper; lovers tracing the shape of an arm or a leg; a rainbow trout swimming upriver. Then everything dissolved into the thin ray of morning's first light, the diffracted prism of time, kingfishers on the bank of a river, sound swirling out of the curved hollow of a lute. She painted to carry these moments across the bridge of time.

Lucinda kept the bedroom windows open, waking each morning with the dawn. She told her husband,

"Something inside me is very free right now." She spent her days painting, rendering the shapes and changing colors of the leaves, birds that came to her feeder, deer eating blackberries in their yard, what she found on the trails as she was hiking up the mountain, and messages from her dreams.

Just before dawn, Lucinda saw a mermaid with green eyes and red hair – the same mermaid who swam through Arianna's dreams. They sat together at the edge of a cove surrounded by high cliffs. When their eyes met, they shared an inner knowing – no need for conversation. Inside a circle of stones, they began to sing – a sweet weaving of voices. Before she swam back to the ocean, the mermaid slipped a palm-size stone into Lucinda's hand – an agate worn smooth by tidal waves and time. Now, the sun was lifting into the sky, creating a river of light from the distant place where the waves began to rise. Time was a river of light, rolling like an ocean wave.

Chapter 18:
The Audition

*A*rianna was preparing to audition for Juilliard, where Janine, her beloved teacher, had studied music. She spent a year perfecting her performance of the Dvorak Cello Concerto, then performed it with the Chattanooga Youth Orchestra. She had already memorized the Fourth Bach Unaccompanied Cello Suite, and she spent hours practicing five Popper etudes with great attention to expression. The audition also required mastery of all major and minor scales, arpeggios and several sonatas. With Janine's coaching, Arianna learned sonatas by Beethoven and Brahms.

Janine, who had become a close family friend, flew to New York with her and shared a room at a small hotel. After dinner at a Japanese restaurant, Arianna admitted, "I'm really nervous about tomorrow morning."

Janine reassured her. "Everyone is nervous before an audition, but I think you'll do fine. I wouldn't have asked you to come here if you didn't play well enough to make the cut. The most important thing tonight is to get plenty of sleep. I'm also going to make sure you aren't hungry. We'll have comfort food for breakfast – something easy to digest. Then we'll walk to Julliard and find a practice room for you to warm up."

Arianna had practiced so much that the music she would perform in the morning orchestrated her dreams all night. The first movement of the Dvorak Cello Concerto took center stage, with the Fourth Bach Cello Suite circling for encores. The Popper *Elfentanz*, "Dance of the Elves," became the soundtrack for memories of cross country odysseys with her family, and somewhere in the early hours before dawn, she fell into a deeper sleep.

Then it was morning, with sunlight reaching through the valleys and canyons of the skyscraper city. Arianna took a shower and dressed in concert black for her audition. Janine put a breakfast of bagels, cream cheese, and slices of banana on the table. She ate slowly, and then it was time to go. They walked to Julliard, through the glass doors and up the stairs, where a proctor was waiting to take Arianna to a practice room to warm up. The proctor let her know she had forty minutes to warm up and then he would knock on the door.

Now, Arianna was alone with her cello. The room had an adjustable chair, like the chairs at the Youth Orchestra in Chattanooga, a music stand, a mirror and a window. Facing the window, she started playing Bach, as the audition would begin with two movements of the Fourth

Bach Cello Suite. She was far away from Signal Mountain, but light through the window helped her feel the spaciousness of the world outside. She felt the connection of her feet with the floor – it helped her stay grounded. And now the Dvorak Concerto, such musical beauty, passion and intensity. Then, a movement of a Beethoven sonata and the *Elfentanz.*

Time condensed and expanded. When she had the sense that it was getting close to forty minutes, Arianna took several deep breaths in front of the mirror. Then she began coaching herself. *I know that I've prepared for this. I've done everything I can to put myself in the best possible space. I know that above all, I love music. I can make people feel the emotions and the joy of the music when I play.*

She remembered the words of her beloved teacher. "When you get in there, think about the music. After all that practicing, don't think about technique. If you're nervous, that's okay. Just stay focused on the music. Your playing doesn't have to be perfect, but it has to be musical."

The proctor, a music student, knocked on the door and asked, "Almost ready?" She took a deep breath. Then she opened the door, holding her cello and bow. The proctor walked her to the audition room and was trying to make small talk. Arianna couldn't respond. It felt so awkward. She glanced at his schedule and found out she was Student #38. A few steps later, he opened the door of the audition room.

Inside, three musicians were waiting – two cellists from the faculty and a violist. They introduced themselves and their names were familiar. She had listened to their recordings. She had heard them play for years. What surprised her most was how friendly and warm they were. They were all musicians she had looked up to, and now, they were ready to hear her play. Actually, she was expecting to feel a lot more nervous, but everything about them made her feel that her presence was welcome.

She adjusted the chair, checked the tuning of her strings, made a small adjustment. She remembered to breathe. Her musical intention was clear – *I know what I want to sound like. I want to enjoy the sound I am making.* As Student #38, she knew that the panel had listened to others playing a similar repertoire and would continue to do that for hours that day. She wanted to give them something enjoyable – something of herself, and hopefully something better than they had heard from other students. One more deep breath, and then she played.

She started with solo Bach. She played through most of two movements, but they stopped her when they felt they'd heard what they needed to. Then they asked for the Dvorak Concerto, and she played part of the first movement before they stopped her. It was one of her favorite pieces and she lost herself inside the music. Next they asked for the Beethoven A Major Sonata and finally the *Elfentanz.*

They thanked her and then it was done. The proctor said she would get the results in about three weeks. Janine was waiting outside of the room, with a warm smile and a hug. She didn't need to ask how it went – she could feel it. After Arianna packed up her cello, Janine handed her a blueberry muffin and a bottle of cranberry juice. It helped her feel more grounded. Then downstairs, out the glass doors, down West 65th Street, past Lincoln Center, and back to the hotel. It was a beautiful sunny day, and she felt such a sense of relief, feeling the sun on her face. She had been preparing for so long, imagining and anticipating. The Dvorak Concerto continued to swirl inside her, and she wished they had let her play through to the finale.

Back in the hotel room, Janine felt she could ask. "I know you played well, but how did you feel?"

Arianna shivered. "It was the longest fifteen minutes of my life."

"Believe me, I understand. Walking with you to Julliard today brought back so many memories."

"I didn't think or worry – I gave myself completely to the music. It was so intense – anxiety at first but then excitement and joy. When I play the cello, I feel connected to everything I love about this world. And now I feel an incredible sense of relief."

Janine poured water into cups they'd bought from a shop outside of the hotel. One had a picture of the Statue of Liberty and the other had the Manhattan skyline with the Empire State Building in the center. She encouraged Arianna to drink. "Let's relax for a little while and then go for lunch. This is something you have worked for, and I know you did your best. I'm really proud of you."

"I still feel flushed and sweaty and hot. I think I'd better take a shower."

"Take your time. No need to hurry."

Janine played Bach while Arianna took her shower. It was something Janine liked to do every day, her morning ritual. Twenty minutes later, Arianna looked more relaxed.

"Better now?"

"Absolutely."

"So now, let's go out and have some fun before we fly home."

By this time both of them were urgently hungry, so they found a small Indian restaurant. Arianna never had tried Tandoori food before, and the buffet let her sample many things – *mattar panir*, *bengan bharta*, *papadams*, mango *chutney*, cucumber *raita*, potato and carrot curry, and Tandoori chicken – all of it an exotic feast. Janine ordered mango *lassi* for both of them, as it wasn't always easy to find mangos in Chattanooga.

After lunch, they walked to the Museum of Natural History to see the whale, the dinosaur bones, the planetarium, and the amazing collection of rocks and minerals. The planetarium reminded her of the stars on Signal Mountain, and she loved the guided tour of the solar system. For dinner, they shared a small pizza with root beer, and then early to bed.

The next day, they took a ferry to the Statue of Liberty and climbed the stairs from the pedestal to the head, with an amazing view of the city and the ocean. At a gift shop, they found a small rhinestone pin of an apple with red, white and blue rhinestones suggesting an American flag inside the apple. Janine bought two of them, one for her and one for Arianna. As she gave Arianna her pin, Janine sighed and spoke quietly. "This commemorates an important event in American history. When I was a music student, the Twin Towers were the tallest buildings in Manhattan. Such a shock when they came down."

The vender caught Janine's eye and said, "I've been

selling hundreds of these since 9/11. For a while, I had a stall across the street from the Twin Towers and I was there the morning they fell. The air was so thick with smoke, I couldn't see out to my hands."

He and Janine shared a knowing gaze. She told him, "I was a student at Julliard at the time. Along with the horror and grief we all shared, it felt like the heart of the City broke open."

"I know what you mean. It was like that for a long time."

Janine sighed. "It's so weird not to see the Twin Towers."

Another knowing gaze. "I feel that way every day. People are still coming to do the circumambulation. There are memories that never disappear."

Arianna knew this was a conversation she would never forget. Later, back in Manhattan, they went up to the observation deck of the Empire State Building and then to Chinatown for dinner. Janine reminded Arianna to put in earplugs before entering the subway.

The next morning, they took a shuttle to Newark Airport, then flew back to Chattanooga.

Chapter 19:

Voice of the Mountains

A few weeks later, Arianna got her acceptance letter from Julliard. After the next Youth Orchestra rehearsal, her parents invited Janine to join them for a celebration dinner in Chattanooga. Jeremy was inspired and felt that his sister showed him what he would do in a few years. He was already planning to follow in her footsteps. He was playing scales and arpeggios in three octaves, playing Bach, and learning the Beethoven Violin Concerto.

Their mother's illness came suddenly. Everything in her body felt suddenly wrong and out of balance. Lucinda's energy disappeared and she had trouble eating. She started losing weight. At the hospital in Chattanooga, the physicians said that it was already too late for radiation or chemotherapy. Home hospice care was the kindest option. Lucinda kept getting weaker.

As the word spread through the music and dance

community, their friends – mostly artists, dancers and musicians – offered what support they could. Every night, someone came to the house with a delicious meal. Musician friends came over with their instruments and played concerts for the family – fiddle tunes and Appalachian mountain music with the folk musicians, beautiful classical music with Janine, her students and friends. Daniel's students came to the house in small groups for lessons, and then they played what they had just learned or improvised for Lucinda. Her artist friends filled her room with watercolor paintings of birds, flowers, dreams, and everything they loved about Signal Mountain.

Daniel and Arianna made soups for her with vegetables from their garden and fed her when she became too weak to do it herself. Arianna played one of the Bach Cello Suites every day for her, and Jeremy wrote music for her after he woke up each morning. Nobody knew how much time they had with her now, but they wanted each day to be a good one.

When she had the energy to walk, Lucinda liked to sit on the deck behind the house and sing. When she felt too weak, Daniel carried her there. She loved watching birds fly to the feeders – every color, every feather. She loved their songs and sang back to them in a gentle call and response. Father, son and daughter listened to her sing, her voice like the mountains. Her voice full of light, the melody drifting through the branches of a catalpa tree.

Daniel did the best he could to be strong for her, but inside, he was crumbling. In his private moments, he was flooded with grief. He did not think "til death do we part" would come so soon.

On their last day together, Daniel held Lucinda in his arms for hours. Their children came in to hug her and play music for her. Just before sunset, Lucinda saw the mermaids waiting. As she closed her eyes, they embraced her and took her home. One by one, her organs shut down until, like a bird, she flew away.

Chapter 20:
Farewell to Signal Mountain

*D*aniel buried his wife on Signal Mountain, beneath the branches of a rhododendron tree. Sun shining through a dark day. The darkness would continue. On lucky nights, he dreamed about his beautiful wife, painting, dancing, making soup, loving him. On lucky mornings, he continued to feel her touch, but then it would dissolve. His children would melt down with tears at unexpected times. Arianna played Bach every night and hoped her mother could somehow hear her cello, carried by birds or angels. Jeremy sat on the back porch and played what he felt on the violin, always in a minor key. He filled a notebook with music, but he was not able to talk about what he felt. He had always been more musical than linguistic. At night, the three of them cooked together. Always, an empty chair at the table. Sometimes they talked about Lucinda and shared happy memories.

Sometimes they focused attention on other things to keep from falling into darkness.

Grief has a way of intensifying feelings, music and colors. Daniel felt that he had to stay strong for his children and for his students. At night, he played the banjo, each night writing a tune to one of his memories. After a few weeks, Arianna moved some of her mother's skirts and dresses to her own closet. Jeremy hung one of her music quilts on his wall, with notes and fiddles moving through a sacred geometry. In May, Daniel took the rest of his wife's dresses and skirts to a barn dance and asked each of her friends to choose one and take it home. Her fabric art would continue to dance that way. For the first time since he lost his wife, Daniel joined the dancers for a square and a few contras. At the end of the dance, however, he refused to waltz with anyone else. That was a sacred moment reserved for Lucinda.

One morning early in May, Daniel woke up with a dream and a vision. He saw himself living on a cliff by the Pacific Ocean. Whether that would come to be or not, it was clear that he had to leave Signal Mountain or he would spend the rest of his life grieving. The dream also made it clear that a life of grieving was not what Lucinda wanted for him. She wanted him to find his happiness again. He couldn't see her when she came to sit with him by the piano or tuck him into bed at night. In dreams, however, she would become visible, hold him in her angel arms, and sing to him. She had so many ways to let him know she continued to love him.

When Daniel shared his dream with his children, Arianna and Jeremy said that if he was moving west, they wanted to come with him. Arianna had become quite inward after her mother ascended. Daniel thought that a new beginning with a new landscape to explore would help her become more involved with the world again. Arianna had three more months before flying to New York for Julliard. She could fly from San Francisco.

During the next few days, Daniel researched music programs in Northern California. He discovered that San Francisco and Santa Rosa had youth orchestras with an impressive repertoire in recent concerts. Jeremy could audition after they decided where to live and continue his studies with a symphony musician there.

They spent the next few weeks deciding what to ship, what to donate, and what to give to friends. They would store their furniture and belongings in Nashville with a moving company that would deliver their worldly goods after they decided where to live. They also let friends in the music community know they were planning to move. One of the banjo players from the Mountain Opry had attended music jams and potlucks at Daniel and Lucinda's home for years. It was his favorite house on the mountain. When he learned that it was available during a music jam at the dance barn, he and his wife made an offer. They made a handshake deal the following Friday.

After the closing papers were signed, the new owners and their children – a family of musicians – helped load the moving van for storage in Nashville and clean the house. On moving day, they gave Daniel a picnic basket loaded with treats for the cross country odyssey, along with a huge mason jar of lemonade and three travel cups. Neighbors came to say goodbye with gifts – a pound of cheese, a basket of strawberries, and a loaf of freshly baked bread. Mid-afternoon, Daniel and his family climbed into the camper and headed north toward Kentucky.

The move to the West Coast was in the tradition of their family summer vacations. They camped every night and played music by a fire after dinner, often joined by families from campsites within hearing range. They were not in a hurry. Each day, they discovered a new place to explore. A lake by a farmhouse, a river with swans, a gallery, a museum, an antique store with treasures from an earlier century. A waterfall, driftwood by the riverbank, close to where the water was tumbling. A profusion of butterflies along hiking trails in the Red River Gorge in Kentucky. A picnic by the arch in St. Louis. A family of deer leaping across the road. A bridge across the Mississippi River, and then the softly rolling hills of Iowa.

While driving, they listened to a weave of fiddle tunes, mountain music, and classical favorites. When one of their fellow campers, also a musician, asked about their eclectic blend of musical choices, Daniel shared a bit of the family history. Yes, they loved Appalachian fiddle tunes, but they had season tickets for the Chattanooga Symphony and both children played in the Youth Orchestra. Turns out, he was talking to an oboist from the Cleveland Orchestra. They talked for a few hours by campfire light, trading musical stories, sharing their love of music and their wishes for their student virtuosi. As the fire melted down to cinders, the oboist recalled a quote by Gustav Mahler: "Tradition is not the worship of ashes, but the preservation of fire."

The musical fire began to burn as Daniel and his family

traveled across the Great Plains. Daniel woke up with music every morning and played it on his violin or banjo. He kept music notation paper in his backpack and let Arianna name the tunes that revealed themselves to him. As they drove, Jeremy made up songs about everything they saw, the way he did when he was younger. Daniel and Arianna added harmonies. Every night, the sunsets across the Great Plains were astounding – dramatic bands of color, cumulus clouds lit with vibrant pinks and fiery shades of tangerine, expanding through an infinite sky. Another kind of holy fire.

The Midwest was humid and hot, with a relentless sun interrupted by thunderstorms, pouring rain and hail pounding the earth as they were driving across Nebraska. Then a profusion of prairie dogs by a truck stop, and finally the Rocky Mountains looming on the horizon. Time to start climbing, and their camper, with its history of driving up Signal Mountain, had the muscle to do it.

Up in the mountains, the beauty was dramatic. They spent a day in Boulder, hosted by a family they knew from a summer music camp. Then a day in Fort Collins with the grandparents of one of Daniel's students. Along Route 70, snaking through the mountains, they stopped to soak in the pools at Glenwood Hot Springs. The next day, they drove to Indian Hot Springs, where they enjoyed the geothermal caves, a hot tub, and a mineral pool. After stopping for ice cream, they found a clearing for their tents, camping with the night sky stretching between carved mountain peaks. Before they went to sleep, a meteor streaked across the sky.

Even though they were still filled with a quiet grief

that persisted as an undertow, regardless of what they were seeing or doing, a sense of adventure took hold and began to multiply. Daniel loved saying yes when one of his children had an idea of where to go next.

"Let's visit the Grand Canyon again."

"We'll do it, and hopefully find another geode this time."

"A magic stone to bring into our new home. And maybe an agate?"

"And after the Grand Canyon, how about Canyon de Chelly?"

"Let's go to Arches National Park! It's close to the Great Salt Lake, which we learned about in school two years ago. The salt flats look like you're walking on the moon."

"Take out the map, and we'll figure out the route."

"I want to see Lake Tahoe and Yosemite."

"We can do that, but then we have to find a new place to live and get you back to school by September." With the summer heat, they decided to avoid Death Valley.

They camped for a few days at Yosemite and hiked the Valley Loop trail, switchback after switchback, through oak woodland to the top of Yosemite Falls. As they climbed higher and higher, they had spectacular views of Yosemite Valley, Half Dome, and Sentinel Rock. The next adventure was a day trip to Tuolumne Meadows, where so many wildflowers were blooming – blue gentians, alpine goldenrod, corn lilies, red columbine, and fireweed. From there, they drove to Lake Tahoe and pitched their tent at the Emerald Bay State Park, with a lakefront campsite. One of the families they met invited them to tour the lake on their boat. The next day, they hiked on trails around the lake and went to art galleries in the late afternoon.

After three days at Lake Tahoe, they began driving toward the left coast. In San Francisco, they stayed at the Youth Hostel by Fort Mason, rode the cable cars, visited the Asian Art Museum, the Academy of Sciences in Golden Gate Park, and the Japanese Tea Garden. They stood in front of the statue of Buddha, feeling a deep peace flowing into them. They watched the koi in the pond behind the teahouse. At the beach by Taraval, they found hundreds of sand dollars and gathered a small collection for their new home, wherever it might be.

Then, in the morning, they started driving up the coast. After crossing the Golden Gate Bridge, they drove to Muir Woods and spent a few hours hiking in the redwoods. One of the Park Rangers told them that Mt. Tamalpais was a sleeping Indian Princess. Yes, they could see her sleeping on a wide swathe of earth, dreaming about the sky. Dinner that night was clam chowder and sweet potato fries at Bodega Bay, then camping by the Pacific Ocean. They fell asleep with the crashing of ocean waves adding timpani to their dreams.

In the morning, they followed the edge of the coast north, often stopping to admire the beauty of the Pacific Ocean and hear the rhythm of the waves. Jeremy told his father, "This is something I would love to hear every night."

To which Daniel answered, "Maybe it's possible. When we get to the right place, we will know."

They left the camper windows open to hear the ocean as they drove up the coast. Gulls and pelicans circled in the distance. What they heard, what they saw made the whole world feel alive. When they drove into Anchor Bay, the magic intensified, so they decided to camp and spend the night.

In the morning, they had breakfast at the Gualala Bakery, then lunch at the Pier Chowder House in Point Arena, with an afternoon tour of the lighthouse. But instead of continuing up the coast, Jeremy wanted to go back to Anchor Bay.

The three of them walked around the shops and especially enjoyed a store that sold crystals, geodes, tiny statues created by local artists, and spiritual books. Arianna asked her father for a small bronze statue of a mermaid, which he bought and gave her. Her presence felt peaceful and contemplative, eyes closed, a smile beginning to form, musing about something others cannot see. She sat on a jutting rock by the ocean, two dolphins at her feet.

In the window of a local realtor, they saw a photograph of a small cabin on a cliff overlooking the ocean. It was by a cove, and the sign said, "For sale or rent." It was before the time that everything became too expensive for a music teacher to buy a house in California. When they went there in the morning, Daniel felt it was the right place to make a new home for his family and his music. His children were enthusiastic. The house would need some repairs, a new roof and new windows, but that was something they could do together. Arianna asked if they could add a deck so they could have meals outside with an ocean view. Daniel and Jeremy loved the idea, and a carpenter who lived down the road had time to help them.

Tim's woodworking skills were at the same high level

Daniel had come to appreciate from the woodworkers on Signal Mountain. He introduced Daniel and his children to their neighbors, including a friend in the roofing business, and advised where to get a good deal on new windows. While the remodel and repairs were in process, they had frequent meal invitations from their new neighbors. Tim's grandmother had grown up in Kentucky and loved hearing Jeremy play fiddle tunes. She asked him to serenade her friends at her ninety-first birthday party, and on beach walks, she taught him the names of ocean birds. Then, after the windows went in, she invited Arianna to sew curtains with her sewing machine. Arianna had packed remnants from Jeremy's music quilt and yardage Lucinda had been saving for future quilts and skirts. She pieced together the curtains in a style that honored her mother's fabric art. Grandma took her for long walks at the beach to look for shells and sea glass and to learn the rhythm of the tides.

One of the gifts of their house was a vintage O'Keefe & Merritt stove, an Art Deco beauty, which they cleaned and shined to restore its former glory. They celebrated with their tradition of chocolate chip and blueberry pancakes on weekend mornings. They hiked in the Mendocino Woodlands and went out for clam chowder at Point Arena. Before the start of the school year, Arianna flew to New York with her cello to start her studies at Julliard. Jeremy auditioned for the Santa Rosa Youth Orchestra, and Daniel was hired to create a music program in two of the local schools. The next summer, he started a music camp to teach fiddle tunes, accompaniment techniques, and Appalachian clogging in the Mendocino Woodlands.

Jeremy helped with the younger children, and Arianna taught bass clef rhythmic grooves to the cellists. Daniel had no idea what his life would be like in the coming years, but for now, he filled his life with music.

The Cove by Anchor Bay

Chapter 21:

The Cove by Anchor Bay

I wonder if the seven sisters of the Pleiades were mermaids. Maybe so, before they flew to the heavens. When I see those tiny stars from a distance, I feel water, fins and undiscovered planets swimming around distant suns. My grandmothers told me that rainbows are mermaid's dreams, shimmering across the sky of our lovely, fragile planet. Other planets have them too. Rainbows are prayers, a promise, a message to follow the hidden longings of your soul, and somewhere, in a parallel universe, angels are listening.

I believe that all women are part mermaid, but not all women are awake to their mermaid nature. Some humans are more awake than others. They are the ones who give sugar water to hummingbirds and savor the rainbows that bless them from the sky. They listen to the messages in their dreams, where angels, mermaids and unicorns whisper. They walk through life quietly as Earth Angels, feeding people who don't have homes and doing what they can to save the planet, which has come into difficult times.

Mermaids whisper to those who will listen, sometimes as distant memories and sometimes as visions of the future. Mermaids and unicorns brought wisdom and beauty to the earth during an earlier time, something the history books are too late to remember. They understood the mysteries in the core of atoms and spoke the language of the stars, a language foreign to most people who live on our planet now. All of the atoms in our bodies were born inside of stars.

The woman I met by the cove at Anchor Bay had memories she could not explain. In her dreams, she had visions of the mysteries and heard music from earlier times. Her intuition was powerful, even though she didn't know how or why she knew. Arianna loved living by the sea. Close enough to hear the ocean tell her stories. Close enough to open her windows and let the waves clear her mind. She loved watching waves flow into the cove in the afternoon. It gave her a feeling of peace, calm and meditation. At night she heard the waves whisper in her dreams.

I can always sense a kindred spirit. One afternoon, I sang an ocean lullaby while I was sitting in a tide pool. Arianna, who was playing music outside on her deck, waved to me, then hiked down to the cove. Her smile was warm and beautiful, and we both have green eyes and long red hair – an interesting coincidence. That afternoon, she started telling me her story, and over time, I began to share mine. She grew up on Signal Mountain, hiking, dancing, playing the cello, and listening to the language of the birds. She plays cello with a string quartet that tours around the country. When she isn't performing, she lives in a cabin on the cliff above Anchor Bay.

Her mother, who left the planet early, was a fabric artist and a painter. She taught her how to make clothes and quilts, how to bake many kinds of bread, and how to find joy in the gifts the world gives you every day. Her mother loved to sketch her while she was playing the cello – sometimes with pen and ink, sometimes in charcoals. Sometimes she used the sketches to paint with water-colors. Arianna keeps the sketchbook of her mother's drawings in her music cabinet, with a few of them framed on her wall. Her father flew to the Spirit World while sun-flowers were blooming late in summer. He comes often to speak to her in dreams, now that he has become one of her Guardian Angels. Still, she misses speaking with him every day, as she did for years before he ascended. She wonders about the stories he never told her, and now it's too late to ask him.

Her favorite neighbor lives in a cabin shaped like a houseboat. Actually, it used to be a houseboat when he lived in Bodega Bay and worked as a fisherman. When he decided to move north, he hauled his houseboat to Anchor Bay and put it on a foundation. Putting it on land was better than scrapping it and cheaper than repairs. He had always lived by the sea. As a young man, he traveled around the world as a radio operator with the Merchant Marines. He told Arianna stories about the food and wine in Italy, temples for gods and goddesses in India, magic carpets in Turkey, geishas in Japan, waterfalls and rain forests in Hawaii, and shamans in Peru. One of the stories he loved to tell was when his ship ran out of food except for wine and communion wafers. That's what the sailors ate until they came to port. Another story was when their Liberty Ship sailed too close to an oil freighter – close enough for sparks, but with the help of mermaids, no fire. The captain was so frightened that his hair turned white overnight while he was dreaming.

When she told me her name, Arianna, she asked for mine. Since I don't have a human name, I asked her what I should call myself. Without hesitating, she said, "You can call yourself Melissa. It means 'honeybee' in Greek. The honeybees keep the world alive when they visit flowers in fields, trees and gardens."

I like the music in the name Melissa. It feels like a name in the Mer language, even though it comes from people above the water.

Chapter 22:

Music by the Water

A few days later, Arianna played her cello on the deck. Beautiful low notes, rolling like the ocean. Something from a human composer named Johann Sebastian Bach. After she saw me, she continued to play – music by Bach and then a melody that reminded me of my grandmothers, notes pouring out of a cave of mysteries. Her music echoed between the past and the future.

After a while, Arianna wandered down the path to the cove and met me by the water. She gave me an apple to eat, and I asked her to tell me stories about her life and about her father. Arianna was quiet for a while, lost in memories, but then began to speak. "My father was the music teacher at my school on Signal Mountain. When I was very young, he taught me to play the cello. I have always loved low notes and beautiful melodies, especially the Unaccompanied Cello Suites by J.S. Bach."

"That must be what I hear you play when I listen from the water."

"Yes, sometimes Bach, sometimes my own music. I often wake up with music in the morning. I'm dreaming, and then the dream becomes music. I hear tones with shape and color, and the music begins to tell me a story. The story weaves a song into the light of the new morning, and my Guardian Angels wake me up so I can write it down. Sometimes the music is for solo cello; other times it's a duet for cello and violin. Lately, I've been getting pieces of a symphony."

"What did you hear when you were waking up this morning?"

"The music I was playing just before I walked down to visit with you. Actually, what I was playing was only half of the piece. It's a duet for cello and violin."

"Violin?"

"It's like a cello but quite a bit smaller, and the notes are higher. My brother plays the violin. Jeremy plays with the Santa Rosa Symphony on the first stand."

"What's a symphony?"

"It's a group of very fine musicians who make music together. Some of the instruments, like the cello, violin, viola and bass, have strings. Others have reeds – oboes, clarinets, bassoons, and English horns. Some instruments sound like birds – flutes and piccolos. Some are made of brass – French horns, trumpets, trombones and tubas. Their bodies are curved like beautiful shells where the music comes out, and they reflect light in a golden glow. There's a percussion section with timpani – they sound like thunder – and other drums, and sometimes a piano, a harp, or an organ. Triangles, cymbals and the celeste have voices like angels, fairies and other magical spirits."

"That's something I'd love to hear. I live in a world of fish, sea horses, coral, kelp and anemones, but sometimes my grandmothers tell me stories about the humans. Some of them went to live among the humans for a while and later returned to the water."

"Is that something you might do one day?"

"I'm not sure if it's still possible. These are stories that happened a long time ago. My people are more ancient than the humans. Some of my grandmothers remember the unicorns."

"You mean unicorns really existed?"

"Of course, but it was a long time ago."

"And what about Atlantis?"

"A wonderful civilization where mermaids and humans lived in peace. During the terrible earthquake, mermaids saved as many people as they could. Some of the people who survived traveled in long boats to Egypt. The mermaids helped the teachers from Atlantis set up a mystery school in Alexandria before they returned to the water, so their sacred teachings would not be lost. Have you ever dreamed about Atlantis? Dreaming is one of the ways humans remember things."

"I had a powerful dream about a water kingdom when I was eight years old. I never told anyone, but I can still see it, somewhere in the middle of the ocean. Other times I dream about traveling to other planets. I see soft, beautiful colors, and life is more peaceful there."

"It's good to know that some of you remember. On our visits to the edge of the ocean, we've watched life change above the water. Species change over time, also the ways of the humans. Civilizations flower, bloom and die. Atlantis, Egypt and Greece. Unicorns, dinosaurs, and so many species of birds. As my grandmother used to tell me, 'If you can't be a unicorn, learn to fly like a bird. If you can't be a bird and soar over the rainbow with magic feathers, better to be a mermaid.'"

"Usually, I wake up with music. It might be a symphony or a concerto I have heard or played, but sometimes it's new. Where it comes from – very mysterious."

"Do you ever dream about the future?"

Arianna was quiet for a while. Then revealed, "I can feel the future but can't find the words to tell anyone about it. Like many musicians, I'm more musical than linguistic. It's easier to express myself with music."

Chapter 23:

The Path to the Cove

*F*or several weeks, Arianna walked down the path to the cove every afternoon to share stories with Melissa. She loved hearing about life under the water, and the ocean was calming. She loved the sound of it, the shapes of the waves, and the way light sparkled the water.

In a quiet way, their friendship was helping Arianna come to terms with her sadness. Sensing this, Melissa asked Arianna to tell her more about her father. It had only been eight months since he left this world. She told her how much she missed him and longed to hear his voice again. She shared stories about her childhood on Signal Mountain, her beautiful mother who blessed her life for seventeen years, and why they had to leave their memories behind. Leaving Signal Mountain was the only way they could move beyond their grieving.

Now, it had been more than twelve years since her mother's passing. Arianna told Melissa about the drive across the country with her father and her brother – vast sunsets above the Great Plains, the rivers that cross the continent, the beauty of the Rocky Mountains, and how the family settled into their cabin at Anchor Bay. As she listened to her stories, Melissa was learning more about the world where the humans live – the geography, the music, and the emotions. It was all resonant with the mermaid world but different in subtle ways.

She had many questions about what she heard. "What was your father's name?"

"Daniel."

"It's a God-name."

"How did you know that?"

"We know how to translate most human languages. A mermaid never knows where she will need to rescue someone or come to shore. Is everyone in your family a musician?"

"I play cello and piano, and my brother plays violin. My Dad played almost everything, but he especially loved the violin and the banjo. My mother was an artist, but she also liked to sing."

"Mermaids love to sing. Our grandmothers sing when we are born. As we grow, they teach us songs that have been sung since the beginning of time. We also make up songs for what we see and what we dream."

"My brother is like that. The next time he visits me, you can meet him."

They were quiet for a while, listening to the waves and enjoying the late afternoon light. A silver line of sunlight illuminated the horizon. Two fishing boats sailed north toward Mendocino. A flock of pelicans gathered around the cove as Arianna continued her story.

"After seven years in California, playing music on the deck, and taking long walks as the tide washed in and out, my father met a beautiful Italian woman named Rosa. One evening, she was sitting alone at Cove Azul, enjoying a plate of clam linguini. My Dad walked in for his Friday night dinner, was taken with her beauty, and asked if he could join her."

Time dissolved as she heard the story in her father's voice.

Rosa was quiet for a long minute, then said, "Yes, I'd love the company." The waitress came over with another menu and Daniel ordered his meal – a cup of clam chowder, fettuccini Alfredo with prawns and mushrooms, and a small salad. As his meal was being cooked, they drifted into easy conversation. Even though they were strangers, something felt uncannily familiar – a smile, an innuendo, a memory, an arc of light. After two hours, they were still talking, sipping hot chocolate with whipped cream from large ceramic mugs.

But when Daniel asked her to meet him for dinner again the next Friday, Rosa became quiet. He could feel her hesitation. He watched clouds of emotion stream across her face, then asked, "Tell me what you're thinking. I want to listen."

Rosa hesitated and then began to speak slowly. "I have to tell you – I'm not interested in dating. I lost my husband a year ago, and I don't want to be married again."

Daniel became thoughtful and was quiet for a while,

lost inside a memory. Then he revealed to Rosa, "I lost my wife many years ago on Signal Mountain. A day doesn't go by that I don't think of her."

"Believe me, I understand."

Then he caught Rosa's eyes and declared, "I have the sense that you have many more years on this planet. You might enjoy it more if you live in the present tense. And believe me, that's something I need to do too."

Daniel pulled out a note pad, tore out a sheet of paper, and with a Palomino Blackhawk pencil carefully drew five lines, a treble clef and a cadence of music.

Rosa was fascinated as she watched. She looked up at him and asked, "What's that?"

Daniel smiled. "It's the beginning of a tune I've just begun to write about you." He wrote his full name and phone number above the notes. "Call me if you'd like to hear it." They had already paid for dinner, so Daniel walked Rosa to her car and said good night.

A few days later, Rosa called one of her friends to talk about the man she had met on Friday night. She kept Daniel's phone number but wasn't sure if she would call him. She described their evening together and was curious about the song but hesitated. "I don't know about this Daniel. I have a feeling that if I start seeing him, he'll be around for a while. He doesn't feel like a just-be-friends kind of guy."

Her friend encouraged Rosa to get to know him. "It doesn't have to be a huge deal – just see who he is. It's been more than ten years since my Chester died, and I wouldn't mind a new companion, even if he's just a friend."

Rosa thought about it for a few more days and then

called Daniel. Their first date was a dinner at St. Orres, where they enjoyed a delicious seafood meal. Daniel reserved a table by a window, so they could watch the wild turkeys on the lawn, enjoy the gardens, and watch the sunset over the ocean. St. Orres had unusual architecture for this part of the world – a castle-like building with turrets, walls of windows, and a view of wild deer from the forest. It felt good to talk to a woman again, and later, to hold her hand. He felt a deep comfort around her and the feeling of familiarity continued for both of them.

Daniel and Rosa met again for a long walk on the beach, listening to the crash of the waves and telling each other stories from their lives before meeting each other. They began seeing each other every Saturday night for dinner, sometimes out and other times at home. Rosa had a painted file box with her Italian grandmother's favorite recipes, and every recipe was full of memories. She had always loved helping her Mom and her Grandma cook, so every dinner came with a family story. Daniel's stories usually began with a tune on the fiddle or the banjo.

Once a week was not enough time together, so they added an afternoon walk each Tuesday, with a few phone calls in between. It became a pleasure to share special events – sometimes a concert in Santa Rosa, especially when his son was playing, a gallery opening or a night of dancing. After four seasons of enjoying each other's company, Daniel asked Rosa to marry him. They had a simple ceremony with his children as witnesses in the Elf Chapel at Sea Ranch.

After many years alone, it was a comfort and a pleasure to have a partner again. Meeting Rosa did not diminish his love for his first wife, but Rosa added joy and sparkle to his days. It was good for both of them to have a companion again, to walk by the ocean, to go to the farmers market for seasonal vegetables, cheese and fruit; or watch a movie holding hands. Rosa's cooking was a daily delight, at times an Italian gourmet feast, and after dinner, she loved hearing the music he played on his violin or banjo. His music lit up her dreams.

Chapter 24:

Mysterious Music in the Water

*J*eremy walked into the cabin with his violin, back from a rehearsal. Mostly, he lived at Rosa's house, since she had reached the point in her life where she could remember her childhood in great detail but could not recall what she did a minute ago. As he had promised his father, Jeremy looked after Rosa's basic needs, made sure she had food in the house and the medications she needed, and drove her to appointments with her physician, a kind man who specialized in working with older patients. Dr. Dorio often took his daughter with him when he made house calls, and Jeremy was teaching both of them to play the violin.

Rosa still remembered how to cook, and she loved going with Jeremy to the market every week. With fish from Point Arena and vegetables from the farmers market at Gualala, she made Italian meals for both of them. Her recipe box was a constant source of inspiration – clam linguini; breaded artichokes; *fusilli marinara* with eggplant, onions and red peppers; shrimp scampi; and Jeremy's favorite – *cioppino*, a seafood stew with clams, shrimp, crab, calamari, rock cod, tomatoes, mushrooms, white wine, garlic and fresh basil. Rosa's favorite dinner was pan-fried petrale sole with butter, lemon, capers and mushrooms. She also enjoyed her Grandma's breaded zucchini, eggplant, mozzarella, tomato and basil casserole, along with her secret family recipe for clam toast. She had learned to cook by helping her Grandma every night. Rosa made salads with arugula, tomatoes, fresh basil, cucumbers and mozzarella, and baked breads swirled with cheese and herbs. For dessert, she served sharp cheddar with apple slices, *cannolis*, or raspberry thumb cookies made with sweet creamery butter. Sometimes she sang as she cooked, usually in Italian, and Jeremy had a black bear's patience when she asked the same question over and over. He watched closely to make sure she didn't leave the stove on.

Years ago, after he moved to the West Coast with his family, Jeremy played with the Santa Rosa Symphony Youth Orchestra. His sister encouraged him to study violin performance at Julliard and helped prepare him for the audition. Jeremy spent four years in Manhattan to study music with world-class teachers, but New York never felt like home. After graduation he lived in Chattanooga for a few years, performing with the Chattanooga Symphony and Opera. Then he returned to Anchor Bay and auditioned for the Santa Rosa Symphony. The conductor put him in the first violin section, and after a few seasons, he moved up the ranks to Assistant Principal. He coached the first violin section of the Youth Orchestra, having been one of them, and gave lessons to private students. He used the Suzuki books with classical technique, but if a student showed interest, he shared fiddle tunes and showed them how to improvise harmonies.

Jeremy enjoyed the drive down the coast and then inland for rehearsals and concerts, a world beyond the stark beauty and isolation of Anchor Bay. One of his musician friends had a large craftsman house with an extra room. He let Jeremy use his guest room after re-hearsals and concerts so he didn't have to drive back late at night. The drive up the coast the next morning was more beautiful, with many places to pull over and watch the crashing waves. Sometimes Jeremy thought about au-ditioning for the San Francisco Symphony, but he didn't want to live in a city. He didn't grow up that way.

When he wasn't rehearsing or performing, Jeremy drove to Santa Rosa, Healdsburg, and sometimes as far as San Rafael for contra dances. He'd grown up clogging to old time bands at the Mountain Opry and loved going to barn dances with his family. Dancing kept him connected with the human race, and in time, provided a circle of friends who were fun to be with. He had girlfriends from time to time, but a part of him always held back. It wasn't something he thought about or even understood, but he was probably afraid that if he gave himself to a woman completely, he would lose her one day, as he had lost his mother that morning on Signal Mountain.

Once a week, maybe twice, Jeremy came to the cabin at Anchor Bay to visit his sister. He still had a room in the house, and they enjoyed playing duets, mainly classical and early music. One afternoon, Arianna invited her brother to walk down to the cove and meet her new friend. When they reached the shore, Melissa swam to them, with her rainbow tail shimmering.

"This is my brother, Jeremy." He was mesmerized beyond the point of speaking.

Jeremy and Melissa couldn't take their eyes off each other. Strange creatures from another world. Lovely creatures with earth and sea colors in their eyes. Mysterious music lifting from the waves.

Chapter 25:

At the Edge of the Water

*N*ow, when Jeremy came to Anchor Bay, he'd play duets with Arianna outside on the deck in case a mermaid or a butterfly was listening. Instead of lunch in the kitchen, they carried a picnic down to the water. Arianna liked sharing food with her best friend, and Jeremy ached to see Melissa. The connection they felt was pulling them like the moon, like the tide, a chord that revealed itself from deep inside.

He came to visit more often now, always with new music to play with his sister. His melodies soared like a warm wind, grounded by the low hum of countermelodies on the cello. Arianna, who had a large improvisational gift, would often suggest chords and arpeggios to add until the music was whole. The music that morning felt like a mermaid's dream.

Every time Jeremy brought his violin to the cove to play for Melissa, new music revealed itself. A haunting melody with the rhythm of waves in the distance. A seagull circling above a cliff. Two seals playing on the rocks and diving into the water. He'd sit on a large rock and play what he heard to Melissa, who listened, half of her body in the sun, mermaid's tail underwater. Jeremy found himself tumbling further and further into a world he did not understand. A world that was beautiful and mysterious. He woke up with music every morning and translated what he heard from the dream world into melodies and harmonies on his violin.

More and more often now, he walked down the path to the water. Sometimes with his violin, sometimes not. One morning, Melissa asked him to come into the water and swim with her. He left his clothes on a large rock and walked into the waves.

They swam together for a while, playing in the waves and above them. No words, just ocean, touch, and salty water. A new season opened and unfolded, with migrating birds, coastal flowers, and warmer weather. In the play of the salty waves, they were in a world beyond time, a world of shimmering joy. Jeremy wrapped his arms around her, and she took him out to sea, further than he had been before. She swam with the ease of an ocean creature, cresting on the waves, with Jeremy riding on her back. Later, they would rest on the sand together, close enough to the water that she could keep her tail in the waves or in a tide pool.

They had so many stories to share – mountains, memories, music, what it was like to live underwater.

What their grandmothers told them. Jeremy's grandmother sang folk tunes and told him stories as she wove patterns on her loom. Stories about the Appalachian Mountains and the people who grew up there. Stories about the secrets of the wind, the trees and the rain, only revealed to those who know how to listen to the mountains. Melissa's grandmothers told her stories of life in coral forests, what sea anemones dream, and the habits of tropical fish – where they swim close to coral reefs and deep under the water. Her favorite stories were about the times when mermaids visited the human world. Mermaids lived for thousands of years, while civilizations rose, flourished and crashed above the water.

Jeremy and Melissa tumbled together, teased each other, slip-sliding up and down her slippery body. Day after day, he was fascinated to hear all about the mermaid world – what she saw, what she knew, who she rescued and brought to shore. He loved playing with her in all the ways lovers play.

Alone at night, he was filled with bliss and salty waves, just thinking about her and remembering where they swam that day. An arm, a swish of scales, her skin, wet and slippery in the waves. Other times, he'd worry about the impossibility of consummation, a joy he had experienced with other women. He knew he could never fully participate in her world, as she had the ability to explore the depths of the ocean while he could not hold his breath that long. Something primitive inside him feared that she would hold him under her magical spell and pull him away from the world he knew.

A dark voice from inside pulled him into undertow.

Could she ever fully participate in my world, on land? Would we always need to be close to the ocean? Could I take her to a concert or a dance? Could she ever come into my house or my bed? Though Jeremy loved to play with her, in quiet moments, he worried about how their different worlds would work over time. But then he would long to see her again and walk down to the cove as the sun was rising. Clearly, he was in water over his head.

Chapter 26:

The Slippery Edge between Two Worlds

*T*he world was getting cold again, soon too cold for a human to be playing in the water. The Santa Rosa Symphony was back in rehearsal, preparing for their first concert of the new season. Jeremy came to the cabin when he could, but other parts of his life were pulling him elsewhere.

When Jeremy climbed down the trail to the cove, Melissa swam to him. They sat at the edge of the water, touching and sharing stories. And since mermaids know how to communicate by telepathy, she spoke openly to his fear.

"I heard my grandmother say that if you carry a mermaid out of the water, she will lose her tail."

"Really? Does it take a long time?"

"I don't know. We'd have to find out."

Jeremy was lit up with the possibility. "I have been longing to share my world with you. There is so much I'd love to show you in the world above the water."

"When I sleep under the waves, sometimes I dream about your world. I hear the music you play as it is coming into being."

"You haven't heard a symphony. Every section – strings, percussion, winds and brass – has a unique sound which speaks in different ways to the emotions. Sometimes the violins have the melody and sometimes harmonies. Sometimes, layers of sound like ocean waves. Each instrument has a different kind of singing, and the composers toss the melody from one instrument to another so you can hear it in different voices. Together, we create something larger than any one of us could do alone."

"It sounds like tropical fish by an atoll, swimming and weaving their colors. Together, they create a rainbow that keeps shifting its shape. Under the water, we hear stories about the human world. How you live, what you love, and the problems you create for one another."

"Do you ever desire to visit the human world?"

"I long for it and I fear it. Sometimes I dream about coming out of the water to see the way people live up there, maybe for a few hours or a few days, and then coming back. But what if I couldn't find the way to return?"

"The world above the water is filled with amazing things, beautiful sights and sounds. You would love the flowers, the birds, and the profusion of stars at night. I know you would love seeing the way light filters through the leaves in a redwood forest."

"But what about your wars? And what about the problems you make for one another? My grandmothers told me the Earth is a Goddess, and many people are abusing her. And doing terrible things to each other."

"Believe me, I worry about these things too, but some of us do everything we can to make the world better. I came to this world to play music, and it would be my great joy to share more of it with you. Symphonies, concertos, operas. The music of this century, music we have loved and played for hundreds of years, and what I play in the morning – the music that comes from the other world."

"I dream about your music."

"In November and December, the ocean keeps getting colder. It will be impossible for me to play with you in the water for many months now. But maybe, if we . . ."

And then it happened.

Jeremy lifted Melissa out of the water and into his arms. He carried her on the path up the cliff. Past lavender, sage and fireflies. Up the wooden stairs to the deck of his home. Into the house.

He filled the bath for her, added a cup of sea salt, and brought her a cup of wild mint tea. He wanted to bring her to his bed.

She read his thoughts. "Let's try it and see what happens."

They spent hours that night in the slippery world. Jeremy was in a trance, in a world beyond music but full of music at the same time, pouring his love into her through his eyes, his skin, his fingertips. And when it was time to dream, they fell into the shimmering between them and merged into the same song.

Chapter 27:
The Mermaid Concerto

*W*hen a mermaid spends more than a few hours out of the ocean, she starts to lose her tail. First a shimmering, then a transformation. At first, it felt like a dream of legs, and then the dream became real. Legs that could only remember their silvery fin in a dream. Without knowing how or why, as sunlight tumbled into the morning, she woke up fully human. Well, almost. All night long, she had been dreaming love songs, soaring and cresting like waves in the salty sea. As every high priestess knows, love transforms the body.

Arianna was surprised to see Melissa at the breakfast table in the morning. Surprised but not surprised. Blueberry pancakes for three that morning and many mornings after. A pot of wild mint tea. Melissa was wearing a Japanese kimono, a gift Jeremy's father had given to his mother. Beyond the wall of windows, they watched fishing boats from Point Arena heading out to sea.

After breakfast, Arianna opened her closet and shared her dresses, as women often do with their best friend. Long skirts flowing with colors of the sea, the shore, the wildflowers, and the cliffs. Silk blouses hued like wildflowers in the garden. A rainbow of scarves to drape over her shoulders. Dresses her mother had sewn and decorated with patterns of quilt work.

"Take what you want," she said.

"So many beautiful colors – it's hard to choose."

"You can choose something new every morning and bring back what you wore the day before."

Melissa chose a long pink skirt, a silk blouse in a deeper shade of pink, and a scarf in ocean colors. Arianna gave her a pair of handmade sandals, but she preferred to walk barefoot unless the ground was too rough for her tender feet.

In the weeks that followed, Jeremy and Melissa began to explore the world together. He gave her a pair of hiking sandals, and they walked the trails on top of the sea cliff. So much to see and feel. He held her hand for connection and balance. Melissa's legs were a bit awkward, like a newly-born deer still finding her feet. At first, she had to limit her walking. She'd stop, rest on the cliffs and gaze at the sea. But in time, her legs got stronger. She continued to wear sandals outside but kicked them off the instant she got back into the house.

Melissa was fascinated by the cello. Low notes that rippled up her spine. High notes that felt like light singing on coastal waters. Grace notes that felt like a new moon. Often, when Jeremy and his sister played music, Melissa added her voice as a descant. Her voice was high, sweet and perfectly tuned. Every day, music flooded into Jeremy, melodies that in time wove together into a piece he called "The Mermaid Concerto." That spring, the Santa Rosa Symphony performed it, with Jeremy and Arianna playing the solo parts. Melissa sat with Rosa in the center of the fourth row, holding her hand.

Living on land was mysterious – so many new things to see every day. Every night, talking and touching, so much to feel and explore. But late at night when she dreamed, she was always back in the ocean, swimming in salty waves, underwater. Sometimes her grandmother's voice returned in a whisper, a far off echo, a wave, a warning. "If you leave our world, even for love, you will never be fully human."

Chapter 28:

In a Parallel, Interpenetrating World

*M*elissa did her best to share her knowledge of parallel worlds with Arianna, who was still grieving her father.

"People don't disappear when they die."

"I didn't think so, but where do they go? I still remember that terrible moment when I knew my father had flown away from his body."

"They fly with birds of light, through a portal to an invisible world."

"What's it like there?"

"They float through a long tunnel filled with light, where they are welcomed by loved ones from the Spirit World. Your mother was there to meet him, overjoyed to see her husband again. At the end of the tunnel, he was embraced by a gentle, loving light, a flow of love and knowledge – what some of the humans call God."

"Does my father have a body there?"

"A different kind of body, made of light, but of course, the same soul inside. For a while, he rests – I can't say how long because time is different there. Then, he meets with a being of light, who you might call an angel, and together, they review his life."

"My father lived a good life."

"Of course he did, and he gets to see it again. During the life review, he sees everything in great detail – his childhood, the day he met your mother, their wedding, the morning you were born. He sees his friends, his students, his teachers, musicians he played with at the Mountain Opry. Beautiful times and challenging times. The angel reveals everything he was not able to see while these events were unfolding. He looks at everything from all points of view."

"I'm sure that will bring a few surprises."

"It does for everyone. From what I've heard, you see all of the people you have loved, the people you had problems with, and everything you have learned. Seeing your memories from the other person's point of view adds a whole new dimension to the experience."

"How do you know this?"

"It's part of the teaching from our grandmothers. Mermaids live for hundreds of years, but when we leave the water world for the last time, we go through the same journey."

"Then what happens?"

"Your father lives for a while in the Spirit World. He enjoys seeing his friends and loved ones again, and since he is a musical soul, he'll play music with other ascended musicians and the celestials."

"Like a symphony or the music we played on Signal Mountain?"

"More like the music of the spheres – ethereal and even more beautiful than the music we have on the earth or underwater. There's a whole group of souls who do this. Other beings paint, and that includes sunsets, the aurora borealis, and the change of the leaves in the fall. Some souls become angels. They watch over the humans and give them messages in their dreams."

"I feel like my father looks after me sometimes while I am sleeping. Sometimes I hear him playing the banjo."

"Everyone has their way of giving signals to the people they love."

"Can he see me?"

"Sometimes yes. Other times he's busy with other things. In time, he will meet with the Snow Angels and decide when to visit the earth again. Where, how, and under what circumstances."

"If humans knew this, they wouldn't be afraid of what my brother calls the Ring of Fire. The day our mother died, Jeremy told me he saw her flying through something that looked like a total eclipse of the sun, high above Signal Mountain, and then into the stars."

"A beautiful vision!"

"Jeremy was only twelve years old when our mother left us. It was so hard for him."

"It was hard for you too."

That night, Arianna had a dream. She was walking to a Japanese restaurant in a city somewhere. Maybe San Francisco or Kyoto. Fog around her feet. She was wearing a kimono like the one her mother wore as she walked through a narrow street decorated with Japanese kites, fluttering dragons, and koi in the ocean-scented wind. A girl ran down the street, laughing with her father. She was eating an ice cream cone and wearing a purple sequin shirt.

Arianna could feel her father in a parallel, interpenetrating world. She walked by the ocean, through a flock of seagulls. A wave broke gently over the stones and shells, with a rainbow in the mist. A warm wind riffled her hair. Now, Arianna and her father walked hand in hand on the beach. The sand was full of tiny jade and jasper pebbles that sparkled under their feet. They watched the waves for a while.

Her father began to play the banjo. A weave of music from the mountains with something she hadn't heard before. Maybe music from the other world? Arianna had been rehearsing Beethoven's Ninth Symphony. In the fourth movement, some of the orchestral chords felt like the music of the spheres. Powerful and ethereal, with one foot in the other world. Arianna wasn't a regular member of the Santa Rosa Symphony, but she played with them when they needed an extra cello. She thanked her father for giving her music. He played another tune on the banjo – mountain music this time.

Everything shifted, drifted apart the way fog does by the ocean, and then they were somewhere else. Her father was jamming with the musical mahatmas, riffing on his bass with Miles Davis and John Coltrane, all of them tossing solos like rings around the moon. Eubie Blake was playing a Steinway on a cloud, his fingers reflected in the shine above the keyboard. They had waited rainy decades to meet again. In the afterlife, they were playing the music of the spheres. Shooting stars, a trajectory of interweaving vectors, voices in perfect harmony. From Coltrane's saxophone, a new universe was forming, a tropical paradise, the delicate tumbling light of a new generation of musical journeys.

Her father hugged Arianna and asked her to remember everything she saw. He reminded her, "The miracle is the moment."

Arianna was suddenly awake. A year ago in the morning, her father had left this world, but she still had the music he gave her and the memory of his voice. She walked out onto the deck and watched the waves rising and crashing. She thought about her father as new light was starting to spill across the world.

Melissa walked out to the deck and said softly, "Over time, his memory will become a source of strength and joy."

Arianna sat on the deck with her memories and a cup of lemon tea. The morning sun reflected in ripples on the waves. Two seagulls circled above the water. Part of her was still inside the dream. *I am left with only today, another morning of light, a gift to be in this world. I wonder if my father sees me today or if he is far away. I wonder what he has learned in the City of Immortality and how it will feel to meet him there one day.*

Inside the tumbling of the ocean waves, she heard her father whisper. She saw his face in a shimmer inside a rainbow, unexpected light.

Now, when she played her cello, she felt that she was

speaking with her father. She'd bring the cello out to the deck and play in the open air. Sometimes an improvisation. More often, something from the Bach Unaccompanied Cello Suites. Today, it was the Sarabande in D Minor. Sometimes, she heard her father's voice between the ocean waves, a whisper from another world.

Chapter 29:

The Farmers Market at Anchor Bay

On Saturdays, Arianna took Melissa to the farmers market. A joy to see so many ripe peaches, berries, and melons. A joy to inhale their scent. Melissa was learning what human beings eat – honey from bees who fly to flowers close to the ocean. Yogurt from the farmer with a herd of banded cows. Pecans, walnuts and almonds from trees in the Central Valley. Cheese from the goats who eat wildflowers on the sloping fields around Mendocino.

The world was a river of color and sound. Seagulls circling over the cove, sage on the hills above the cliffs, butterflies with tapestry wings in the garden. Ribbons of light delivering gifts to her eyes. Time expanded and condensed. She had a wisdom older than the redwood trees and eyes that saw the world as if newly born. The world was singing to her, every leaf and flower filled with light.

Most afternoons, she returned to the ocean for a while. Swimming in the cove, the fish were still her friends. They swam to her and shimmered her arms and legs. The kelp waved in an underwater dance. Sea turtles carried their tapestry shells through time. The creatures who lived underwater knew her mermaid name – not the name the humans called her.

Night was always a mystery, warm and inviting. Often, Arianna, Jeremy and Melissa ate dinner by the sliding doors to the deck. They lit candles and served their meal on apple blossom glass plates and bowls, with placemats woven by Lucinda. Their table was the one Daniel brought with him when he moved to Signal Mountain. They made soup with miso, ginger and vegetables from the farmers market, always delicious with fresh bread and cheese. Jeremy savored the whole process of kneading and baking bread. Often, he rolled the dough with herbs and cheese. Other times, he added layers of dried fruit and nuts.

While they were sitting by the cove one afternoon, Melissa asked Arianna if she hoped to meet a soulmate. Melissa was lit up with love – a joy and a mystery she wanted to share with her sister. From what she had seen so far, love was core to the human experience and maybe the best part of the world above the water.

Without hesitation, Arianna answered, "I have a soulmate. I haven't met him yet, but I will. When humans become involved with someone who isn't right for them, it brings pain. I'd rather wait, the way my parents did."

"Have you seen him in a dream?"

"I do often. My Guardian Angels won't let me see his face, but they tell me things about him. A musician, for sure. A man of integrity. They tell me some of our friends already know each other, but we haven't met. When I daydream about meeting him, I see a gathering of musicians and dancers in a redwood forest. A music and dance camp in Mendocino or Santa Cruz. Jeremy and I go to dance weekends sometimes. More often than not, he goes as a staff musician and I go as a dancer."

"Jeremy tells me that dancing is one of the ways people meet each other."

"It is, but some people go for the pure joy of dancing. Contra dances have live music – sometimes a local band and sometimes a group of traveling musicians. I go for the music and because I love to dance, but I wouldn't mind meeting someone special on the dance floor."

"For you, it has to be someone really special."

"I know I have a soulmate. Sometimes I feel him looking for me. I hear him playing music, half of a duet, and sometimes in the morning, I know the other half of the melody."

"Do you write it down or remember it?"

"In this notebook. I'm going to need it one day."

"Do you ever feel sad about not meeting him yet?"

"When I feel lonely, I play music to call him in. When the time is right, our circles will touch. Until then, I'm happy to enjoy my own company."

Back in the kitchen, Arianna began preparing a salad in a wide maple bowl that a woodturner on Signal Mountain had given her parents as a wedding gift. There was so much family history in the wood. She spread a bed of arugula for the first layer, then steamed red and gold beets. When she sliced them, Melissa said they reminded her of sand dollars. For the top layer, medallions of goat cheese, dried cranberries and honey-glazed walnuts. Melissa made a miso soup with sweet potatoes, spinach and leeks, and they sat to eat by the window.

Chapter 30:

The World Dreams in Music

*J*eremy and Melissa were always touching. Like sun and water. Silver moonlight on the waves. Every night, Melissa loved him the way a mermaid loves. Waves and salty water, overflowing with joy.

Jeremy loved sharing music with her. Every night he would choose music for dinner, mostly classical. Sometimes World Music or Appalachian fiddle tunes, but mainly classical music he had played – Beethoven's Ninth Symphony, Brahms' Fourth Symphony, Brahms' *German Requiem*. Tchaikovsky and Mendelssohn. They listened to several Mahler symphonies, and then he took her further back in time with Mozart's piano concertos and Bach's *Toccata and Fugue in D Minor*. He guided her through Dvorak's *New World Symphony*, movement by movement, explaining the influence of African-American spirituals, jazz from New York City, and Native American chants.

"What is it like in New York?"

"Crowded, noisy and very exciting. Tall buildings and more people on the sidewalk every day than you would see in a month in Anchor Bay. Subways in tunnels below the city. Amazing exhibits in museums, art from all over the world. Crazy people singing between the trains. Amazing wealth and terrible poverty. Too many people – you wouldn't like it there."

"Did you ever live in New York?"

"I lived in the West Village while I was studying music at Julliard. I took over the sublet Arianna found when she was a student – a fifth floor walk-up apartment on West 11th Street. My two favorite neighborhoods in New York are SoHo and Greenwich Village. SoHo is full of artists' lofts and art galleries, and the Village has always been a haven for poets, artists and musicians. Try to imagine Arianna walking up five flights of stairs, carrying a bag of groceries and a cello. The apartment had a tiny living room with a window, a kitchen and a bedroom with a loft to sleep in. You had to climb up a ladder to get to the bed.

"I stayed with her when I auditioned for Julliard – she had camping pads and a quilt for a guest bed on the living room floor. By the time I started my studies at Julliard, she was touring with her quartet. They performed in Europe for a few years and then began to travel around the United States. Arianna and I shared the apartment, but she wasn't there a lot of the time.

"After graduation, I went back to Signal Mountain to spend the summer with my friends and audition for the Chattanooga Symphony. They placed me on the third stand of the first violin section, and I performed with them for the next few years. What an amazing experience to be on the same stage, playing with musicians I had admired for years! Some of my friends from Julliard auditioned for the New York Philharmonic and other major orchestras, but it's really hard to get in. I didn't want to live in a city so I didn't try."

"Did you live in Chattanooga or go back to Signal Mountain?"

"I shared an apartment in an old house in Chattanooga with another musician from the Symphony. We each had our own room, which we needed to practice and rehearse. On days off, we liked to hike on Signal Mountain."

"A woman or a man?"

"A woman, very talented oboe player. We were close friends, but it wasn't romantic. When she went on dates, I let her know if I thought the guy was good enough for her or a player."

"What's a player?"

"Someone who goes to bed with a lot of women."

Melissa looked agitated, her face covered by a dark cloud. "In the mermaid world, mating is for life."

"Humans aren't always that way. Some people like to be sexual without a commitment. Other people seduce their partner into believing they are serious when they're really not."

"Isn't it obvious?"

"It could be, but sometimes people see what they want to believe and ignore the other signals."

"Not wise."

"It leads to a lot of pain. But sometimes, when people

get involved, they don't know each other well enough to know if they have a future."

"Humans should pay more attention to their intuition."

Jeremy ended the conversation by putting a CD in the player. "I think you'll enjoy this – the Popper *Requiem for Three Cellos and Piano*. My sister performed it at Julliard with three of her friends." After that, he chose the Beethoven *Trio in C Major for Two Oboes and English Horn*. "My roommate in Chattanooga played this at a concert. She was very talented."

"Where is she now?"

"She moved to New Orleans to play with the Louisiana Philharmonic Orchestra. Maybe we can visit her. New Orleans is an amazing place."

"Yes, I know. I was there with some of my sisters after Hurricane Katrina. There wasn't a lot we could do, but we rescued a few of the children who lost their parents."

Arianna, who had been reading a book on her rocking chair, started to pay more attention to their conversation. She caught Melissa's eye and said, "Do those children still remember you?"

"If they think about it, it feels like they're having a dream. It's not something they can tell their friends, but inside, they know. Once you have an experience like that, you never completely go back to the ordinary world."

"I understand. It's hard for children when they can't share what they know with their friends."

"We swim into their dreams from time to time so they don't doubt themselves."

"Young musicians have the same problem. They tend to be out of phase with the other children, except when they are with other musicians. A football player is not going to understand their gift. When Jeremy and I were growing up, our friends were the music kids."

Melissa was thoughtful, then smiled. "Humans are funny sometimes." She ate a papaya and watched the sun falling into Anchor Bay. She lit a candle, then asked Jeremy, "When did you move back to Anchor Bay?"

"I played with the Chattanooga Symphony for three years, but I kept feeling that I should spend more time with my father in Anchor Bay. With parents above a certain age, you never know how long they will be around. Just before Thanksgiving that year, I flew west to audition for the Santa Rosa Symphony. Some of the musicians already knew me from the Youth Orchestra, and they welcomed me. After the audition, they put me on the second stand in the first violin section. After three seasons, I was moved to the first stand as assistant principal."

"Why not principal?"

"That chair was already filled. Anyhow, it's more work being principal. You have to do bowings for the whole section, mark the parts, and prepare the solos. Before the first rehearsal, you have to be ready with everything, and you don't get a chance to rehearse before you are leading the section. Some people need to be principal. When I have the opportunity, I enjoy it but I don't need it."

Jeremy turned on the radio to listen to a live broadcast of the San Francisco Symphony. The three of them drank tea and listened to Mahler for the next two hours.

When she was alone, Melissa liked to listen to the radio. She enjoyed learning what people did around the world and what they discovered, although the news usually horrified her. She sampled various types of music, with a strong preference for what was melodic and gentle. She liked songs that told stories. She especially loved "Fields of Gold" by Sting. It told her so much about a world she had not experienced before. Every new song was fascinating. "Operator" by Jim Croce. *What's an operator? Telephone booth? What's that?* "Time in a Bottle." *Now that's an interesting concept.* "Smooth Operator," by Sade. *Why do humans use the same word for different meanings? That must be another word for the player Jeremy told me about.*

One of the best ways to learn about humans was to listen to their songs.

Chapter 31:

Rosa Ascends to the Spirit World

*R*osa died peacefully in her sleep, during the full moon in November. She had been dreaming about her husband, climbing a mountain toward a star in the far distance. He beckoned her to follow, and she flew out of her body, away from this world. Jeremy found her resting gently on her bed in the morning when he arrived with a bag of oranges and fresh baked bread.

As soon as Jeremy let them know, Arianna and Melissa walked to Rosa's house. They sat with her for a while, then washed her body in salt water. They dressed her in silk and scattered rose petals over her. It was clear that she was no longer there, but they wanted to honor the clay that had carried her for so many years. Outside, a gentle rain made the world shimmer.

Back at the cabin that night, they felt Rosa's presence

but mainly kept silence. Since it was their habit to listen to music while they prepared their meal and ate, Arianna put on Brahms *German Requiem*, which she and Jeremy had played at Julliard. Brahms composed the *Requiem* for his mother, and more than a century later, his music continued to comfort those who listened. Later that night, the *Requiem* continued to weave melodies, chords and harmonies through their dreams. Just before dawn, Arianna had a powerful dream about Rosa and her father. As soon as the morning light touched her eyes, she reached for her journal to write it down.

The door opens on Tuesday. On Friday she walks away from the world. I saw them at the Symphony, Brahms and one hundred voices around them. He was wearing a black suit with a top hat, she in a long silk evening gown, his arm softly around her shoulder. They waved at me from a high window and then they walked into the stars.

Nobody else could see them but they waved at me from a high box in the air. In the fortissimo, low pedal tones of the organ vibrated the ceiling and the walls, and in the quiet moments, one hundred voices hummed the chord of the earth as it turned.

In another world, she is skating on a river, in the rose pink of sunset or dawn. A fox fur hat around her face keeps her warm, sheltering her as a cottonwood tree from thunder. These memories comfort as a soft pillow, green and cool, a meadow glowing with wild irises and daffodils, the path through the forest where she walked, where the leaves of her life glow like rhapsodies at her feet.

The next morning, brother and sister began to attend to the details of a parent's passing. Jeremy would keep Rosa's house and Arianna would keep the cabin by the cove, since he and Arianna would need separate houses if either decided to marry. Rosa's home was filled with beautiful things – Persian rugs, sculptured Italian lamps, and Murano glass. In time, they would decide what to keep, what to sell, and what to donate. They arranged for the cremation, and three days later, they scattered Rosa's ashes into the cove.

Chapter 32:
The Notebook

*I*n an old trunk in the house where Rosa and her father had lived, Arianna found a notebook. The cover was red leather, with elegant ivory pages and thin brown lines. Opening to the first page, she saw the distinctive handwriting she recognized as her father's. Slowly, she looked through the pages. Story by story, she discovered a journal he had written for more than thirty years. Not every day, but when he had something deep to share. It was full of memories of her mother, along with the part of her father's life he hadn't shared with her before, from the time her mother ascended and they moved to Anchor Bay, to the time he met Rosa.

At the end of the notebook, he had written a waltz for Jeremy and a letter to Arianna, followed by a waltz he hoped she would play at her wedding.

My darling daughter,

Between my two marriages, I took seven years to explore how I might live on my own terms. I had a few women friends, and from the start, I let them know I was not planning to settle down with anyone. Your mother and I were soulmates, and I knew I would not find that depth of love and understanding with anyone else. After a long and loving marriage with two children, I was not ready to be part of another family.

I know you have taken the years you need to find yourself, and you listen to your own music. But you also know the great happiness I shared with your mother and found later in my life with Rosa. Every year was sweet, each one of them a blessing. My wish for you is to find your love. And my toast to you when you meet him, "May you be as happy as we are."

This notebook has stories for a memoir I planned to write. I was going to call it *Branches*. I know you will find it at the right time.

With great love,

Dad.

Arianna spent the next few weeks reading her father's notebook. Her favorite pages were those he wrote after she was born and a poem he wrote after he met Rosa. She also loved his memories of hiking on Signal Mountain, teaching young musicians, and playing music at the Mountain Opry. During the years between his marriages, he had grown to love his freedom and had been struggling with this when he wrote the poem.

Paradox

For Rosa

For seven years
I loved my freedom.
Any threads that bound me
Were chains of iron.

I broke the chains
And reveled in freedom.
Freedom was life;
I was reborn.

Then I found you.
The sparkle in your eyes
Was my beacon
Guiding me to love.

You gave me your love
And I was again a man.
I am now free but bound
By threads of moonbeams.

Arianna went out to the deck and watched the waves. She thought about her life in the light of her father's vision. Yes, full of music, some very special friends, but romantically empty. She thought about the soulmate she had sensed but hadn't seen. He came into her dreams but was never there in the morning. She wondered how long it would take to meet him. In that moment, she became more open to the possibility.

Chapter 33:
One Thousand Stone Steps

Melissa went for a swim as the sun was setting, enjoying the change of light until the moonlight shimmered the cove. When she was ready to return to land, Jeremy held her hand as they walked the path that zig-zagged up the cliff, one thousand stone steps in the moonlight. They had the cabin to themselves for a few weeks while Arianna was touring with her quartet. Jeremy was preparing the Saint-Saëns Violin Concerto No. 3 for a performance with the Golden Gate Symphony in San Francisco. When he was learning a concerto, he liked to play it every day until he had it memorized, with every passage under his fingers. Melissa was fascinated by the process and the subtle ways the concerto kept getting more and more passionate and beautiful.

She sat in front of the fireplace and watched the shape

of the flames. She loved falling asleep with Jeremy's arms around her, waves rippling in her memory. The day was for living on land, and night was for the world underwater. All night, she dreamed inside salty ocean waves. Dreams of lantern fish, coral castles and tropical islands. Rainbow sails billowing through time. Visions of earth and oceans revealed themselves. The history and the future of the planet. What Jeremy saw in her eyes – the ocean of time. A shower of light. A new moon ready to reveal its secrets. Their love nights, silky and wild. A thousand kisses.

In the morning, they watched the sunrise, light awakening after the earth was dreaming, silvering the waves. Rippling water shining like pearls. Jeremy saw the changing shapes and colors as a dragon in the clouds.

"Or a seahorse," Melissa said. "Sometimes I feel like I'm dreaming the earth and the water."

But sometimes at night when the world was quiet and Melissa was sleeping, Jeremy would lie awake. Tiny waves of doubt and worry rippled through the music in his mind. *I love Melissa more than I've loved anyone, but is she the one my soul has chosen? I have lived on the Earth for twenty-eight years. She has lived for more than 300 years, mainly underwater. Could she give birth to a child, and would that child be a human or a mermaid? What if I ask her to marry me and then she goes back into the sea?*

One night, after a very disturbing dream, Jeremy took his violin and went outside to the cliffs. Melissa's grandmothers whispered in her dream. They draped a necklace of pearls around her shoulders, and when she woke up, her bed was empty. She walked to the window, then went out to the deck. Moonlight was streaming on the cove, over turbulent waves. She saw visions in the patterns of light over rippled water.

In the moonlight, she saw Jeremy on the cliff, playing his heart out to the waves. Mysterious music she had never heard before. The melody and the way he shaped his vibrato made her arms shiver. He was so full of music that her heart was taken out to sea.

Chapter 34:
The Tide Pool

Melissa and Jeremy were sitting at the edge of a tide pool, legs dangling, touching toes. They were feeding each other slices of papaya. A starfish had attached to a rock. A pentagram, a messenger. Melissa had begun to crave more and more time in the water.

Jeremy had been waiting for the right moment to talk. "I've been wondering . . . I've been reading my father's journal about the time before Arianna and I were born and what it felt like for him when my mother was pregnant. My father was so deeply in love with her, and it got even stronger while we were growing inside her. I want to feel what my father felt, and in my dreams, I feel the presence of a soul who wants to enter the world."

Melissa closed her eyes for a while, then opened her eyes and looked deeply into Jeremy's soul. "I can feel the soul of the child, but I'm not sure that I'm his mother."

When Jeremy started the conversation, he didn't know what to expect, but it wasn't this. "Have you ever thought about having a child?"

"Not really. Not everyone in the Mer world has children."

"Would you at least consider the possibility? You and I are at the point where two humans deeply in love might get married and have a child."

"But not all human couples have children, and one of us is not human."

"And one of us is not Mer." A long silence followed before Jeremy spoke again. "I know that your grandmother fell in love with a man who lived on Bali. Did she marry and have children?"

"She is so much like me. She rescued his son, who had been carried out to sea on a tidal wave. He was on a bamboo raft in the open ocean, and she carried him to land. His mother was never found, so my grandmother lived with Hanuman and his son for many years."

"Any more children?"

"No."

"They loved each other, but she never felt entirely at home above the water. She was a young woman then, very beautiful, but she never felt that he loved her as much as he loved the boy's mother. One night, her grandmothers held council in a dream, and in the morning she returned to live with them in the water."

"Do mermaids always return to the water?"

"In every story I've heard, but it might not happen during your lifetime. Mer people live longer than humans. Thousands of years. As time goes on, your hair will be woven with silver. Your body will change in many different ways. My body will stay much the same."

"Will that bother you?"

"Why should it? Change is part of life. In the Mer civilization, we don't worry about time the way you do."

"But here's my real question. If we decided to have a child, would the child be human or Mer?"

"I asked my grandmothers the same question. They said it cannot be predicted. Like what you call the toss of a coin."

"That's a very big risk – for both of us."

"It was one of many reasons why they didn't want me to come here."

"But they did it. Why wouldn't they want you to do it too?"

"That's the point. Something bad happened, and my grandmother would not give me any details."

"Did you ask?"

"Many times. The only thing she would tell me is, 'Never trust a human.'"

"Do you feel that way?"

"It's something I struggle with. All of those human songs – 'Smooth Operator,' 'You're So Vain,' 'Long, Long Time.' You have always seemed different than the men in those songs, but sometimes I don't know what to think."

"How can you love me if you don't trust me?"

Chapter 35:
The Line between the Worlds

*A*fter a moonlight swim, Jeremy wrapped his arms around Melissa, holding her close and warm. But he couldn't stop wondering, "If we have a child, will it be human or Mer?"

"No way to tell in advance. My grandmothers never expected this of me."

"Can you ask in your dreams? I know you can sometimes see the future."

"I have asked, many times. No messages. I asked the prophesy stones, but the stones are silent."

"I keep having dreams about being a father, and they show me a beautiful soul waiting for an invitation to be born. When I ask, my Guardian Angels don't tell me whether the baby has feet or fins."

"When you dream about having a child, your soul is speaking."

"But what if you leave? What if you both leave?"

"If the prophesy stones are silent and my grandmothers won't speak, they are leaving it to us to make a decision."

"Nothing is logical here, but let's consider both sides. If the baby is a human?"

"I will stay here, with both of you."

"If a mermaid?"

"I'll have to take her back to the water, so she can breathe and receive her education. Baby mermaids have to live in the water. In the human world, children who are different are tormented by other children. A different skin color. Too skinny or too smart. And a tail? That will never work in the human world."

"A lot of parents teach their children at home."

"In the Mer kingdom, the grandmothers teach the children."

"I'm starting to feel a line between our worlds that we were never meant to cross. Humans are bonded powerfully during birth. We love our children and want to hold them. We want to take care of them and teach them everything we know about the world. I couldn't bear to be the father of a child and then lose her."

"Or him. It's going to be a him."

"Did your parents take care of you when you were growing? You never talk about your mother. Is she still alive?"

"She is, but she swam to a different part of the world. Close to Thailand. People there needed our help when refugee boats were escaping from Vietnam. Many people would have perished without our help. My parents liked the people they met. The Vietnamese have proverbs like, "Learn kindness first, words later." My parents had wonderful stories to share when they came back to visit. But then there was a tsunami in Sumatra, and they had to leave again."

"Did you miss them?"

"I've always been closer to my grandmothers. It's like that in the Mer world. After children reach a certain age, the parents have their freedom. We love our parents and they love us, but taking care is the responsibility of the community."

"Hard for me to imagine. When I grew up on Signal Mountain, we did everything as a family. Hiking, meals, summer travel, Friday nights at the Mountain Opry. We grew a lot of our food and cooked it together. We went to museums and concerts in Chattanooga, and we played music together at home. The day my mother died was the worst day of my life. I couldn't talk about it for a long time."

"Have you ever talked about it?"

"Not really. I didn't talk to anyone for a while; I was too sad. I know my Dad was worried about me, and he made an appointment with the school psychologist. When he told me about it, I refused to go to school that day. I took my violin into the forest and played for the trees. When I think about my beautiful mother leaving, all of the pain comes back. When I get close to a woman, I'm always afraid that she'll leave too."

"Then what happens?"

"It's only been a few times, but something about her really starts to bother me."

"So you leave before she can leave you?"

"You know too much about me."

"I think we understand each other – well, as much as I can understand a human. And if you do what you always do, you will create the same future."

"Did you ever love a man in the Mer world?"

"No."

"Why not?"

"I never met anyone who felt like a soulmate. If you remember what I told you about the sailor on the Isle of Inishmore – there was something about the way that sailor looked at me after I rescued him. He frightened me, but there was something in his eyes. I'm not sure what it was, but so different from the Mer world. Even though I swam away, something deep inside me wanted to love a human."

"And that's why you came to shore?"

"I dreamed about it so many times. My grandmothers tried to warn me not to do it, but I had my own ideas and my own dreams."

"My beautiful dreams are about music, and my terrible dreams are about my mother leaving. Sometimes I dream that you will leave too."

"I'm not your mother. I'm not planning to leave you."

"But when you talk about returning to the sea . . ."

"I'm not ready to do that. This is my home now, with you."

"What would your grandmothers say? Sometimes I know they're calling you."

"If they knew what you were dreaming, they would tell you to ask for different dreams."

Chapter 36:

The Language of Music

*M*elissa liked tuning into the music of the world. When you know how to listen, everything above and below the water is singing. She thought about her name – Melissa, like the honeybees who delighted her in the garden. Their buzzing held an echo of the murmur of the sea. Wildflowers delighted her. They were like rainbows in the sky and fish in tropical waters. The violin Jeremy played reminded her of the singing of dolphins. She wondered how much longer she would stay above the water and when she would return to the sea. Dreams of her grandmothers were coming more and more often now.

But the Earth still had mysteries she longed to explore. For a few weeks, she traveled with Arianna and her quartet, all women from Julliard. On their concert tour, they played quartets by Beethoven, Brahms, Mozart, Dvorak, Borodin, Taneyev, and a new quartet by Matthew Arnerich, a gifted composer from Santa Rosa. Arnerich wrote music that was contemporary but also tonal and melodic. He loved beautiful melodies, unlike some 20th century composers who preferred to be jarring or layer sound without a clear melody.

Melissa had a hunger to learn more about music. One morning, Arianna put a cello in front of her, showed her how to hold the cello against her body, like an embrace, and how to hold the bow.

"Like this?"

"Relax your hand. Not a grip – a hold." Arianna adjusted her hand. "More like a baby's hold. They are strong but flexible."

She showed her how to play the open strings. "No pushing or pressure. Scoop the bow into the string to get more sound." She demonstrated and asked Melissa to listen. Then she used too much pressure and asked her to listen again. Then back to a bow stroke that produced the sound she wanted. Melissa heard the difference and tried again. Arianna smiled. "Yes, better."

"What about vibrato? You make it look natural, but it doesn't look easy. What's your secret?"

"There are many things you'll need to learn and practice first, but when the time comes – lots of repetition. A hand that is both relaxed and controlled. Vibrato is the way you shape the sound, but it's not something you learn until you've been playing for a while."

"When you sing, I also hear vibrato."

"I try to base my playing on the human voice. Every

morning, I listen to three different singers when I do my morning stretches. The human voice, accompanied by an orchestra. I also listen to the great cellists – Mstislav Rostropovich, Yo-Yo Ma, Pablo Casals, Jacqueline du Pré, Alisa Weilerstein, Gautier Capuçon. To my ear, the human voice always wins, in terms of quality, beauty and depth of sound."

"Sometimes your hand looks like a hummingbird's wings, and sometimes slower."

"If you only have one kind of vibrato, you can't be as expressive with it. If I want to express passion, I use a wide vibrato. If I want to have an intimate, tender moment, I use a smaller, narrow vibrato. If I am expressing joy, I use a medium width, medium speed, or sometimes faster to give the joy more energy."

"I love the way you move when you play the cello."

"I move out of sheer enjoyment. I'm dancing with the music."

All morning, Jeremy had been practicing the Tchaikovsky Violin Concerto for the Mendocino Music Festival. Melissa planned to go there with him and asked what it felt like to play a concerto in front of a large audience.

"It's a physical thing, but it comes from a place deep inside. My heart is going a million miles an hour, but inside, I'm in touch with something deeper – a primordial sound, drawing from infinite silence. The music moves from self to wood, and then through the f-holes. I like to offer my music to everyone listening as a gift."

"Can you feel the people listening when you play?"

"When someone listens deeply and carefully, I can feel it, but not everyone listens that way. Most of the time, I'm totally inside the music. It's a place of joy and wonder, and every time I enter, I'm grateful and amazed."

Arianna, who had been drinking tea in the kitchen, walked over to where they were sitting and joined the conversation. "It's kind of a Zen experience. You practice and practice. Then, when the concert comes, you show up and do it. At that point, I stop thinking about technique and give myself totally to the music."

Jeremy agreed. "Human beings need music to be human. To create beauty. To be in touch with the highest aspirations and longings of the human soul. Music is more of the language I speak than English. Music is my love language with the world."

Melissa was still not sure what it meant to be human. It was something like being a mermaid but also different. And where was the fine line between the mermaid and the human? Under the water, she knew a different kind of singing.

When both musicians were touring or rehearsing, Melissa had time to herself to explore the world and time to think about the world in her own language. In the early morning, birds sang to her as the world began singing. She watched the sunlight awaken the morning with colors emerging out of the night's shadows. When she walked outside, the wildflowers on the coast were singing. She loved watching the way calla lilies unfurled and how light feathered through ferns in the forest. She loved the redwood trees – they held the history of the planet. Manzanita stretched red, spindly branches through the morning. Birds flew to the branches, and soon, the whole world was singing.

Chapter 37:

The Singing Circle

*M*elissa sat by the ocean, weaving her voice with the water. Light on the waves, rippling out to distant islands. Jeremy walked out to listen. The Santa Rosa Symphony performed music by local composers, and he wanted to find a way to put what he was hearing inside a symphony. It was a different kind of sound that he could not easily describe. Not the whole and half step intervals of tones he learned in music school. Not modal or chromatic. He had begun composing his first symphony, *Voices under Water*, with a choir in the second and fourth movements.

A whale surfaced and spouted in the distance. Then another. Jeremy wanted to find a way to bring the presence of whales into the music. Melissa kept singing during their morning walk and she sang to the whales.

Jeremy was fascinated by the sound of Mer singing and wanted to know more about how Mer people learn to sing.

"We sing in the music circle with our grandmothers – a language we learn easily as Mer children. Our music wraps around the sonar of whales and dolphins, and they understand our thoughts."

"Are there any Mer children who can't sing or can't hear the pitch?"

"I don't think so. We listen and match the sound. Let me sing for you my grandmother's favorite tune."

Jeremy knew in that moment that what he was hearing would be the core of the final movement of his symphony – first with a soprano soloist and then weaving through the chorus with a theme and variations. He was thinking about the way Mahler used glissandos to slide down the strings in his early symphonies. That might be a way to hit the tones Melissa sang between the usual intervals of Western music.

The shore was littered with driftwood and sea glass, perhaps from a storm somewhere, but the sun was gentle on their skin as they walked. He was fascinated by her mastery of so many languages, enamored again and again by the beauty of her voice. He slipped his hand into hers. Melissa continued to sing and a tiny bird flew to her hand.

Melissa had been thinking about Jeremy's question. She asked him, "How do humans learn to sing?"

"Some children learn from their parents, especially if their mother or their father sings them lullabies. From the time I can remember, my mother sang me a lullaby every night, and my Dad played a tune on the fiddle or the banjo before I went to sleep. Some children learn from their grandparents. Some children learn from their friends, or in school, or by listening to the TV or the radio. However, there are humans who can't match pitches or sing in tune."

"Really? That seems so strange to me. Nobody ever taught them how to listen?"

"Evidently not, but my vocal coach at Julliard feels that everyone can be taught to hear and sing. It's a matter of ear training."

"My grandmother would like him! In the Mer world, everyone sings. We sing melodies and weave harmonies, the way coral weaves underwater."

"How do you learn so many languages?"

"We just listen."

"Humans can learn languages that way, but only when they are very young children. It gets harder as they grow."

"It's hard for me to understand this. When we travel to different places, we listen deeply and soon we know the language."

"A few humans have this gift as adults, but not many."

"Something I've been thinking about – you keep asking me to stay here. Have you ever thought about coming with me back into the water? If we had a Mer child, maybe you could live in the sea."

"You can return to the water any time you choose. If I stayed underwater, I'd drown. I wouldn't grow a Mer-tail or a fin."

"I never asked my grandmothers if a human can become Mer. It's something I've wondered about, many times. I know you could learn the language. It's very musical."

"But if I had to stop playing the violin, I would die."

"Oh no! I should have thought of that. But if we have a child, we'll have to do what's right for the child, regardless of the sacrifice."

"The thought of losing both of you is just too much for me."

"If he's Mer, I could bring him up to visit you by the cove."

"That would never be enough!"

Chapter 38:
The World Lit Up with Her Singing

*N*ow, every night when she was dreaming, Melissa returned to the water. Jeremy knew – he could feel it. Sometimes the music of her grandmothers came in a whisper, then in a cresting wave. Water-filled notes, banded fish, weaving together in an iridescent harmony. Jeremy heard water music in his dreams. He heard the mermaids singing, high pure notes. He saw Melissa swimming to him in warm, salty waves, and the world lit up with her singing.

But would he wake up from the dream one morning? Was this the life he was meant to live? Was it real or was he dreaming?

Mermaids and humans live in different worlds, even when they love. Like most mermaids who come to land, Melissa's legs were not always steady. She liked to spend part of every day in the water. When Jeremy took her hiking in the redwood forests of the Mendocino Woodlands, he had to walk slowly and steady her sometimes.

He had tried a few times to teach her how to dance, but her legs were still too awkward. They were a new possession, not fully accustomed to this world. Water ballet was easy, but not dancing. When he took her to a contra dance, she loved the fiddle tunes, but she preferred to sit on the side and watch. The winding, tinny notes of the banjo reminded her of seaweed, and the notes of the string bass felt like ocean waves. The way the instruments wove together and played with harmonies reminded her of tropical fish swimming around an atoll. For Jeremy, fiddle tunes reminded him of the mountains where he grew up – the singing of trees, owls in the moonlight, hiking under the stars.

One afternoon, he took Melissa to the Lighthouse at Point Arena and then to the Pier Chowder House. He enjoyed a bowl of corn and seafood chowder, and she ordered a baked potato. She would not eat anything from the sea. The fish and the mollusks were her friends, and sometimes she missed swimming with them.

The Prophesy Stones

Chapter 39:
The Dance of Opposites

*H*e didn't know why it happened, but one morning Jeremy woke up feeling restless. It was a feeling he recognized and had felt before with other women. First, a whisper of discontent, then louder and more insistent. Emotions like an early April wind, wanting to rain. Legs that wanted to run down mountain trails he remembered and explore the valleys and rivers of his childhood. Dreams that wanted to raft a new river, hike to the summit of a new mountain, and follow the chords of a melody waiting to be born.

Jeremy began reading everything he could find about mermaids, the way a child who has come close to a tornado becomes fascinated by storms. He uncovered myths about enchanted women singing to sailors to lure them to their death, stories of mermaids growing legs on land

and losing them again in the water. He found legends of mermaids bestowing kisses with magical healing properties – yes, he knew those kisses. He read every story about mermaids he could find, in a desperate attempt to make sense of his life with Melissa and its mysteries.

Stories of mermaids circled the globe, and Jeremy was fascinated by when and where they emerged from their watery world. Of particular interest, when they were helpful to human beings. And how, after living many years on land, they disappeared. He read legends of the selkies from the Northern Isles of Scotland, seal-women with long flowing hair. The only way to keep a selkie on land was to hide her sealskin. Melissa had lost her mermaid tail in the passion of their love nights, but could she transform herself again?

Jeremy had been feeling shadows in his heart, and it made him wonder if Melissa was feeling her own shadows. Mermaids are so beautiful in their loving. They whisper gifts of higher love to the men with whom they share their secrets. They touch with a divine tenderness – yes, he knew that tenderness – but later they return to the water. Always back to the water. This was something he could not bear, not after opening his heart this way. As he walked with Melissa along the rocky shoreline, he found himself trusting and doubting at the same time.

Since mermaids are telepathic, she knew, but she tried to distract him. She told him stories about swimming with migrating whales and lantern fish swimming in deep ocean caves. She told him the mermaid story of how the world was created, from the womb of the Cosmic Mermaid swimming in heavenly waters, and how all of the stars and planets were her children. She told him her grand-mothers' stories about the mermaids who swam near Irish villages, enchanting traveling bards until their Celtic harps played music that sang like stars. She shared stories about mermaids swimming with dolphins as they carried a small boy to shore, with a gift of a shell or a pearl.

Late at night, she led him to the place where light merges into water and dream. They swam to visions of jeweled rocks and coral islands. They heard music that rippled through time. Jeremy's emotions were a flock of seagulls flying through each other and disappearing in opposite directions.

Sometimes he wondered if he was dreaming all of this and when he would wake up. There were things about being a mermaid he would never understand, and aspects of being human that he could not explain to her. In time, would this create an unraveling? Sometimes he was filled with joy and amazement, but he spent too much time wondering what was real. Some of his dreams were on the earth and some of them in the water. His mind had become a mysterious dance of opposites.

By the time the season turned, Jeremy began to doubt everything. He was filled with a desperate longing to live a life that was more fully human. He kept wondering whether a mermaid could give birth to a human child, and whether the child would live on land or water. Fear flooded his emotions, a green tide taking over what he knew in his heart. He used orchestra rehearsals as a convenient excuse to spend longer and longer times away from his home in Anchor Bay. But how does anyone return to the world after loving a mermaid?

Chapter 40:

Dancing in the Kitchen

*W*hat is it about human beings and the way they love? Melissa heard whispers among her Mer sisters that humans stay in love for only a short time. After that, the honeymoon needs to be transformed into something deeper. A second wave, and then a third. The unraveling starts with little things that annoy, often the same qualities and quirks that delighted in the beginning. Jeremy had always been good at beginnings, but could he find a way to enter the second wave? In the Mer world, love is eternal. Mating is for life.

Melissa woke up in the morning quietly humming songs filled with dolphins, ocean waves, and the whispering of her grandmothers. Jeremy woke up grumpy more often than not. But sometimes, his dreams took him back to Signal Mountain, where he danced in Appalachian barns with his parents and his childhood friends.

On those enchanted evenings, his mother was still alive, dancing and smiling. So much of him had been shaped on Signal Mountain. He knew there was a large contra dance community in Northern California. Melissa had shown him worlds he could not imagine before he met her, but he felt he was losing part of himself. And why was he seeing the glass half empty instead of drinking the wine that had been offered?

Jeremy wondered how it would feel to take Melissa to a contra dance and get her out on the dance floor instead of sitting on the side. That night after he fell asleep, he played with the old fiddlers at the Mountain Opry. Bluegrass banjo and fiddle tunes, bass thumping and vibrating the walls. Very sweet dream. Later, he waltzed with an old girlfriend, twirling her in a skirt his mother had designed. Dancing was something he had shared with all of the other women he had loved.

On Saturday morning, Jeremy woke up humming a fiddle tune, music with memories of Signal Mountain. He picked up his violin and began to play it. From an invisible parallel universe, his father accompanied him on the bass. Arianna heard her father playing from somewhere unseen, and she added chords and harmonies with her cello. Her heart was filled with joy.

Later that morning, Arianna went outside to gather peppermint from their garden and brewed a pot of tea. Jeremy made chocolate chip pancakes with blueberries from the farmers market. Everyone was humming and singing. Melissa put a vase of sunflowers on the table, stems and petals leaning out of blue glass. Between pancakes, the three of them continued a vocal improvisation. After breakfast, Jeremy took out his violin and started riffing on fiddle tunes. He and Arianna tossed the melody back and forth, adding rhythm and harmonies. Then he started clogging on the kitchen floor. One thing Jeremy knew, he was going to the contra dance that night in San Rafael. He invited Arianna and Melissa to go with him, but Arianna was not enthusiastic about the long drive home late at night. She had a rehearsal in the morning. "Melissa . . .?"

Melissa was quiet for a long time.

Jeremy offered his request as a ray of hope. A shimmer of light on the ocean. "Melissa, won't you come with me? Dancing is so much fun, and you've been living here for almost two years now. Maybe your legs have gotten stronger. Give it a try!"

Arianna joined the conversation. "Contra dancing is easy – I think you can do it. Anyone who can walk can contra dance. It's just moving to music, and you love music."

Jeremy was hopeful. "We have new people learning every week, and they always have a lesson before the dance. How about if you try just one dance? The first one is always easy. Let me show you a few of the steps."

In the kitchen with Arianna, he showed Melissa a few of the simple figures – circle right, circle left, forward and back. Slowly, a right hand star. Left hand star, circle left, forward and back. But when he showed her how to swing your partner, even though he moved slowly, Melissa lost her balance and fell to the floor.

Jeremy picked her up and hugged her. Melissa decided to try again, but Jeremy was worried. Most of the figures weren't hard, especially in slow motion, but during the swing, even in slow motion, her legs wobbled. Again, she stumbled and fell. She sat on the floor and remembered what her grandmother said, that she would never be human. Her eyes filled with tears.

From the floor, she looked up at him and slowly, sadly said, "I can't do this. I'm so sorry."

Jeremy searched for words. "I didn't want to upset you. I just want to share something I love with you."

"I know how to dance, but we do it in the water. Have you ever danced with a dolphin?"

"I can't say that I have."

"You're really missing something special."

They walked out to the deck and sat in silence for a while. A flock of pelicans was flying south in their seasonal migration. Three fishing boats sailed toward Mendocino. The wind picked up from the ocean. Jeremy still wanted to go to the dance that night but didn't want to leave Melissa home.

"Honey, why don't you come with me? Even if you don't dance, I know you'll love the music. The band that's playing tonight is one of our best."

"Something inside me is telling me not to do it." Slowly, quietly, she told him, "As much as I would love to share this with you, my legs just won't do it. It's the only part of my body that hasn't fully entered the human world."

"I don't mind if you're a little bit awkward. At every dance, there are always new dancers. You won't be the only one."

"But they will learn and get better. My legs will never be as steady as I wish. They still have memories of the water. They will not come with me when I return to the water one day."

This was exactly what he had feared, what he had read about in so many stories. Melissa felt his fear but could not help him.

Jeremy sighed. "I guess I'll stay home tonight."

"No, you should go to the dance. I don't want to keep you from doing something you love."

"Are you sure?"

"Jeremy, if you need to dance, go dance. If I need to dance, I'll do it in the water!"

A few hours later, he drove down the coast toward the dance in San Rafael. He had an invitation to stay overnight with musician friends in Santa Rosa if he didn't feel like driving back to Anchor Bay late at night. He'd see how he felt after the dance. A mile down the road, driving south along the coast, a green wave washed over his emotions. He wondered if there were other parts of his soul he couldn't share with Melissa, and if these things would matter over time. Below the water, the mermaid grandmothers were watching.

Chapter 41:

Fiddle Tunes on the Dance Floor

*W*hen Jeremy walked onto the dance floor that night, it felt like coming back home. The fiddle tunes were in his blood, full of memories of his childhood. He was not looking for love inside the tribe of contra dancers, just the wild abandon of moving that way. Changing partners every dance gave him a sense of community, and he gave himself to the miracle of the moment. He was new and mysterious on the dance floor, and it was clear to anyone who watched him that he had been doing this for a long time. Every woman in the room wanted to dance with him. At the end of the last waltz, after an amazing sequence of twirls and flourishes, he dipped his partner to the floor. When the music stopped, he twirled his partner one more time and escorted her back to her friends. Then he put on his shoes and walked out the door.

On the long ride home, Jeremy had to be honest with himself. His time with Melissa had been an amazing love affair. An astounding gift, but something about it didn't feel right anymore. She was not going to be his wife.

Jeremy had reached a point where he could not bear living with someone who would never be human. And how to tell someone he loved that she was not the one his heart has chosen? That would not be easy. With Melissa, he had discovered a way of loving that goes way beyond what most humans are capable of – a mermaid initiation that had totally changed his life from the core of his atoms. But now that her way of loving was woven into his heart and his body, couldn't he share it with someone else?

Riding along the winding roads on the cliffs by the Pacific Ocean, Jeremy found himself longing for communion with one of his own kind. Melissa would never be able to dance. She would never be able to hike at his pace or run down a mountain. Something about her legs, new arrivals to her body, didn't want to move that way. And what was most important – he knew he wanted to be a father one day. He wanted to share his music with a new generation, and he kept feeling the soul of a child who belonged to him. His emotions, like waves on moonlit water, rippled and dissolved. Neither he nor Melissa knew if a child born of a mermaid would stay on land or return to the water. Dancing was really not so important. Yes, a great pleasure to dance with someone you love, but many dancers have a favorite partner for dancing while sharing the rest of their life with someone else. But not knowing whether his child would have the ability to live with him was an issue that could not be resolved.

As he was driving North, Melissa had uneasy visions in her dreams. She was on the land and then underwater. A flow of seahorses, a predator fish. A child walking into the ocean, then riding on a mermaid's slinky back. The constellations twirling to an earlier place in time. A sailor drowning, a swirl of colorful fish, a shower of falling stars. The sailor on the Isle of Inishmore was reaching for her hand. She was swimming away from him as Jeremy slipped into their bed. Now, she felt the warmth of her grandmothers' voices, welcoming her back home. But was the time past, present or future? And what was time, anyway?

More and more, Melissa's dreams took her back into the ocean. She swam in a forest of coral at night, enjoying the filtered light of the water. Jeremy continued to be restless, except during love play on the beach or in their bed with open windows, their arms and legs lit by moonlight. Mountain music and butterflies from the trails on Signal Mountain traveled between their dreams. The moonlight left a trail of pearls on the beach, leading back to the water.

At night, Melissa's grandmothers swam around her and whispered in her dreams. In lilting, ethereal voices, they sang the wisdom songs that mermaids have known since the beginning of time, melodies full of waves and ocean. They left pearls of moonlight shining on her pillow and pearls that floated on the water as they began to light a path back to the life that she had known. But when dawn light floated through the window, Jeremy's arms were around her and she could feel his dreams too – waves crossing each other with countermelodies, motifs of a symphony or a concerto he would write one day. Jeremy's dreams were always full of music.

Even with her grandmothers' whispers around her, Melissa kept searching for new ways to please him. Jeremy loved to dance, but this was a world she couldn't enter. In dreams, she saw him on the other side of a window. A dance club filled with human women in colorful dresses and slinky shoes. Could she find a way to break through the glass? And would it wound her spirit, along with injuring her beautiful hands? She knew her legs would never be human, but her hands were beautiful, on land or water. They didn't age like a human woman's hands.

The closest thing she could find to dancing was water ballet. It was easy to move gracefully in the water. At Arianna's suggestion, she started coaching a troupe of synchronized swimmers who were preparing for the Olympics. After swimming with them for several weeks, the whole troupe took on a distinctively mermaid feel. She showed them new ways of moving and helped them design mermaid costumes that shimmered in the water but still gave their legs the freedom to move. Humans needed that. She also suggested music that sounded like her grandmothers' singing and worked with a local composer.

Jeremy was amazed when he watched them practice. It was mysterious and beautiful. He didn't understand that she was doing this to please him. Inspired by the grace and beauty of what he saw, he decided to challenge himself in a new way, by taking ballroom dance lessons. It would give him the opportunity to dance with women who understood what it was to be human.

Chapter 42:
Mermaid Ballet

A few weeks later, Jeremy and Arianna joined Melissa to watch her synchronized swimming team in a pre-Olympic trial in San Francisco. Melissa had not revealed much about the choreography – she wanted the water dance to speak to them without an introduction. After a drive through Golden Gate Park, Jeremy left Melissa at the door of the new gym at San Francisco State University and then found a parking space by Lake Merced. Melissa went to the locker room to join her team, stretch, and put on her costume. After walking back to the campus, Jeremy and Arianna found seats on the benches by the new Olympic pool. There was a hush and then applause as the team emerged.

As he watched the mermaid ballet, Jeremy was astounded by a level of power and grace that for most humans would not be possible. He knew the choreography was Melissa's, and at the insistence of the women on the team, Melissa swam with them. It was like watching the corps de ballet set up the stage for the entrance of a prima ballerina. Melissa entered the water ballet with a backflip and sideways spin, twisting herself in the air and arching her back as she entered the water. Jeremy had never seen anything like it. Melissa leapt out of the water like a dolphin. She swirled like a school of fish, rippling the water. She was a contortionist twisting her body into shapes and positions that normal people could not, in or out of the water. Then the corps de ballet followed in perfect synchronized patterns. In their mermaid costumes with an emerald green sparkling tail, something about the way they moved felt like a vision from a fairy tale. Everyone witnessed a choreography never before seen in artistic swimming.

Jeremy was mesmerized to the point that he could hardly speak. After the roar of applause, he said to his sister, "I had no idea that Melissa could move like that."

Arianna leaned over to Jeremy. "She may be the one who puts them over the edge into the winners' circle."

Jeremy recognized the music from melodies Melissa had sung to him. That was the biggest surprise. Other teams had routines choreographed to hip hop. This music was ethereal, beyond space and time.

After the performance, Melissa was swarmed by admirers. Jeremy and Arianna took the opportunity to speak with other women on the team. Arianna asked one of the women how she felt about going to the Olympics.

"I'm a person who loves difficult challenges. I believe in the power of passion to achieve your highest aspirations."

Her friend was equally enthusiastic. "If you want to be the best, you have do what others are not willing or able to do. I keep seeing our team with gold medals."

Arianna was inspired. "You're going to get there. I know it! When I see you on TV during the Summer Olympics, I'm going to remember this day."

Jeremy was curious about their training. "I see a lot of ballet in your movements. Do you all dance as well as swim?"

"It's part of our training. The Russian team has trained with the Bolshoi Ballet, so we did something similar – world class training with the San Francisco Ballet. The way we move our hands, our arms and our legs above the water comes from our ballet training. At the Olympics, the judges look for a team that is clearly dancing in the water. The Russians are the defending champions, and we intend to beat them this year."

"Will Melissa be going with you?"

"She isn't sure yet. Celeste is her understudy."

Jeremy moved through the crowd to find Melissa. Gathering her close and then gazing into her eyes, he shared his amazement. "Your swim team does honors to the mermaid civilization. What I just witnessed is better than anything I saw during the last Olympics."

"The water holds me. It's where I'm most at home."

"Do the other women on the team know you are a mermaid?"

"They've noticed that I can't do everything on land that I do in the water, but most of them feel it's a handicap I have overcome. Other women on the team have healed from injuries and trauma."

"Will you be going to the Olympics with them this summer?"

"It's possible, but I don't know where I'll be living at that time."

Jeremy fell silent. He wondered if dancing in the water had developed her leg muscles to the point that she could move more gracefully on land, or if water ballet would take her in an uncharted direction. Maybe she was just being stubborn, or maybe she knew more about what was inside him than he realized.

A few nights later, Jeremy lit a room full of candles and put on a CD of waltz music with all of his favorite contra waltzes from touring bands. Her legs had to be getting stronger from all the swimming. Maybe if she could waltz with him, she could take another step toward being human. Melissa knew his heart had become restless. Had they lived inside a magic spell for the past two years? How was it that now the spell was broken? Melissa felt the distance and had been contemplating a return to the water.

Jeremy and Melissa sipped lemonade with slices of strawberries filling the bottom of the glass. They listened to music and watched the flames in the fireplace. Without hesitation, Jeremy swept Melissa into his arms and began the slow circles of a waltz. He moved slowly and carefully as Melissa gazed into his eyes. She was able to take long walks along the shore, had been able to do that for many months now. But something about the circular movement of the waltz put her off balance.

Jeremy kept her from falling and lifted her into a hug. As she hugged him, he twirled her around the room, then set her down on the sofa and tumbled next to her. It had been an ecstatic moment for both of them, but his vision of taking her to the dance on Saturday night tumbled down the cliff and slid into the water.

Jeremy put his arms around her and held her close. He kissed her tenderly. She knew what he wanted, and they both knew it was something she could not share.

Chapter 43:
Au Coquelet

*J*eremy drove to a contra dance once or twice a month. Sometimes in San Rafael. Sometimes in Santa Rosa. Nobody knew anything about him except that he loved to dance. He came alone and left alone, which sparked rumors. One night during an open band in Berkeley, he took out his violin and began to improvise with the featured musicians. He knew every tune they played and added harmonies, descants and countermelodies.

For the last waltz, a woman with brown eyes and wild curly hair asked him to be her partner. Jeremy was intrigued. He led her onto the floor and then into ballroom position, surprised by the cutouts on her dress at the waist and halfway up her back. His hands touched skin. As they circled around the dance floor, he enjoyed the waterfall of her raven hair. He led her into twirls, a lean at the end of a phrase, and a dip. She was radiant in the swirl of her dress, low cut with beads, pink netting and silk.

At her request, they went out afterwards to Au Coquelet for a pastry and a cappuccino. They shared a few stories as he gazed into her dark mysterious eyes. Tanya was intrigued when he told her he played with the Santa Rosa Symphony. She said she would come to see him at his next concert. He was intrigued when she told him she taught dance at studios in San Rafael and Cotati. She had performed in the Nutcracker when she was in high school, but now her passion was tango.

"In the mountains where I grew up, everyone knew how to clog and square dance, but nobody knew the tango."

"Certainly, you've seen it in movies!"

"A few times . . ."

"And . . .?"

"It's a very sensual dance, but I've never thought about learning how to do it."

"Actually, doing it is far better than watching. Would you like to try? It's easier to learn with a partner who already knows the moves."

"I would enjoy that. Artistically, I've been wanting to stretch myself."

"How about Saturday night?"

Chapter 44:

Two Can Tango

*T*anya and Jeremy made plans to meet at a night club in Cotati for a tango lesson and an evening of dancing. They met half an hour before the lesson to claim a table, order a glass of wine, and stretch. The teachers came from Argentina, and the musicians were visiting from Buenos Aires – a quartet of violin, piano, bandoneón and bass. Around the room, small round tables were covered by pink cloth, set with a votive candle in red glass and a red rose.

Tanya's legs were long and sinewy, like any ballerina. Her feet were strong and supple. Her dress, rose red, slit halfway up her thigh. Two red roses adorned her hair. Her eyes said, "Come to me and I will show you secrets."

Jeremy reveled in the body to body telepathy, slinky and sensual. Clearly, Tanya had the soul of an artist, but she was firmly rooted to the earth. Yes, that's what had been missing. Until now. They danced for almost an hour and then returned to their table to watch the other dancers. Jeremy moved their chairs to the far side of the table, where they leaned together to share observations about the other dancers. Tanya pointed out subtleties of their style, as dancers she knew passed by their table. Other times they sat in silence, knees touching.

The pianist had wild curly hair and musical telepathy with the other musicians and the dancers. The woman who played bandoneón was on break from a famous club in Buenos Aires. She swayed with the music as the string bass vibrated the walls with rhythms so sensual that the room was bathed in a visceral eroticism. The violinist played Piazzolla favorites, along with original music.

Watching the other dancers was like visiting a cabaret somewhere back in time. Jeremy admired the style of a dancer in salmon spike heels, her silky tangerine dress slit to the top of her thigh. Her partner could have been dancing in a movie or in a brothel in Argentina. They were very skilled, performing *ochos*, dips and leans, leading up to a stunning lift.

Another couple was wildly dramatic. He was wearing an Argentinian vest and a red silk shirt. She was wearing black lace over a red silk camisole and slip. Her lipstick, bright red, scented with the memory of wild nights in Argentina. A red rose in her hair, and her beautiful leg in fishnet stockings now swept over his thigh. He twirled her, dipped her, and with skillful hands, lowered her to an arch and slid her across the floor.

Tanya led Jeremy back onto the dance floor, to practice the moves he had learned during the lesson and show him a few more. He held her close in her beautiful red dress, and he felt like taking it off. Later, when they were alone, he could not control himself. They drove back to her cabin in Lagunitas and spent the night in loving embrace. An ocean of desire. Clothes scattered on the floor with a river of moonlight flowing through the window.

Chapter 45:

Breakfast in Lagunitas

Jeremy's dreams were edgy that night. All night, a dream of a turquoise river rippled through his sleep and continued to whisper in the morning. A rainbow trout studded with jewels, swimming upstream, back to spawning grounds. Her back and her fins dripping with ropes of pearls and precious stones. Mysterious music returning to the light where it was born.

He continued to hear the music in the morning, with an early December sun shining on his bare shoulders. Quietly, he left the bed, found a sheet of paper and a ruler, drew the lines of a musical staff, and began writing the music he had been given in his sleep. When Tanya awoke, she was curious to hear the melody, but his violin was in his bedroom in Anchor Bay.

Tanya was disappointed, but he told her, "I'll play it for you the next time I come to see you. I'll bring my violin."

She found this reassuring but sensed a hint of moodiness. Since she had only known him for a few days and then had known him intimately, she wondered about his mood and where it was coming from. She brewed coffee, a French roast from Good Earth Natural Foods, and put some raspberry scones on the table. Also a bowl of tangerines.

Jeremy was lost in the music for a while and then stayed quiet. The melody kept revealing itself and he continued to write what he was hearing. Tanya was not comfortable in the silence, so she began a conversation. She asked if he slept well and shared her dream, something about dancing below a waterfall high in the mountains. Jeremy shared his dream about the turquoise river and the music he heard, how it was still haunting him. He told her about the way music comes to him in the morning, and then he was quiet again.

"I love the violin and look forward to hearing you play."

"Do you play a musical instrument?"

"When I was younger, I tried a few of them. First the recorder, then the viola. Our school had a good music program, and we could try a few instruments. At that time, I was also taking dance lessons and dreaming about joining the children's classes with the San Francisco Ballet. My parents didn't have enough money for dance lessons and music, so they told me I had to choose. I loved to dance so the choice was easy."

"My father was my music teacher. He was the one who taught all of the kids at school, and he gave us lessons at home. I grew up playing music."

"What an amazing gift!"

"One of many gifts. We were very close, and there isn't a day I don't think of him."

"How long has he been gone?"

"Three years now."

"I can't imagine being without my parents. Does it get easier over time?"

"I still miss him, some days more than others."

"My parents live a few miles down the road in Fairfax. I'm lucky that way."

Jeremy got quiet again. He drifted between worlds – the kitchen, the music, Signal Mountain and the cabin by Anchor Bay. He thought of Melissa singing on the balcony and walking by the water.

Finally, Tanya asked, "Jeremy, you seem to be here and not here at the same time. Perhaps I detect a hint of sadness? I'm not exactly sure why, but you have me wondering if you're involved with someone else." She did not want to further extend her heart if her heart would break.

Jeremy hesitated. "I don't know exactly how to explain this, but I'll try." He spoke slowly. "For almost two years, I've been in love with a mermaid. She is lovely and mysterious, but we can't completely enter each other's worlds. I don't feel that we have a future together."

"A mermaid? What exactly do you mean by that?"

"A beautiful woman from the sea."

"Can you tell me more about her?"

"I'd actually rather not. It's not working out, and I've been trying to figure out how to free myself."

"Is she a dancer?"

"She's not, and it comes between us at times."

"But surely she has other qualities you enjoy."

"That's what makes it so hard. I love her and I know I have to leave her. Have you ever met a man who was amazing but just didn't fit with your life?"

"That happened about ten years ago and it was hard to recover. I was head over heels, and he didn't feel that way about me. It took a few years before I was even willing to see someone else."

"Any involvements since then?"

"Only casual. A few dance partners. Some coffee dates and a friend with whom I go to the ballet a few times a year. It's not romantic. Nobody else has captured my heart that way."

"But are you ready to love again if you met the right man?"

"Yes, absolutely. And you?"

"I would hope so, but it may take a while."

"What about your mermaid is wrong for you?"

"It's hard to put into words. I've been trying to explain it, even to myself. One thing I know. I would like to be a father one day, and she is not the mother of my child."

"Hmmmm." Tanya felt a hint of relief, but still felt agitated.

Jeremy saw the cloud that swept across her face. He was not sure what he could say to reassure her, so he said what was on his mind. "Sometimes, life is an enigma."

"I guess I need to ask. Are you available, or not?"

"Available. I'm doing what I can to free myself."

Tanya did not believe in mermaids and did not understand the story Jeremy told her. She thought he was speaking in metaphors.

Chapter 46:

Meanwhile in Anchor Bay

*M*elissa and Arianna went out to the deck for breakfast – strawberries, yogurt, granola and slivered almonds. Melissa looked tired and agitated, which was not usual for her in the morning, and said, "Did you notice that Jeremy wasn't here last night?"

"I'm not sure what's up with him these days. He's been so moody."

"Moody and annoying."

"Something has changed inside him, and I don't like it. Even though we grew up together, I don't feel like I know him anymore."

"He isn't as open as he used to be."

"Unfortunately, you're getting more experience of what human women go through on this planet."

"I'm a mermaid. Even without my tail and fins, I will

never be human. If this is what it's like to be a human, I'm going back to the ocean."

"It upsets me that my brother is acting this way."

"Love is different in the Mer world."

A shiver went up Arianna's spine, along with a powerful intuition. She kept it to herself.

Melissa had been learning to play the cello. Arianna had her practicing scales in two octaves, along with some etudes – what children play when they are learning. She used the Suzuki method, teaching Melissa to play by ear and then memorize what she learned. The shift to reading music was gradual. Arianna brought a student cello to the house so they could play duets – a cello she named Lolita. She had chosen the cello carefully – it had good tone and was easy to play.

"Let's stop thinking about Jeremy for a while. I want to teach you how to do a trill so you can start learning the Bourrée from the Bach Cello Suite in C Major. I think you're ready for that now."

Melissa liked to practice and had been progressing. Arianna had recently given her the *Feuillard Method for the Young Cellist*, which was full of duets for students to play with their teacher. This had become a daily activity.

They warmed up with two duets, first an Etude by Romberg and then a Larghetto by Handel. Arianna watched Melissa's hand, her bowing and her face. She saw a shadow that hadn't been there before and a sadness. After the duets, Arianna took out the music for the Bourrée. "Let me play it for you first." Playing Bach every day was part of her spiritual practice, and the Bourrée was an old friend. "Now, slowly, you can play it. I'll play it with you the first time." She showed her how to do a trill, first slowly and then faster. "And if you want to embellish, this is where you add a tiny trill."

Melissa played it again, and Arianna smiled. "Excellent! Now you can practice."

Melissa still had a shadow on her face. "I love playing the cello. I will miss it when I return to the sea."

Another shiver ran up Arianna's spine. "I think both of us need a vacation from my brother. I'm leaving for a short tour with my quartet tomorrow afternoon. How about if you come with me?"

"I'm coaching the swim team in the morning, but we can leave after lunch."

"We'll bring both cellos."

Chapter 47:

Two Cellos, a Quartet and a Mermaid

*M*elissa swam in the morning while Arianna packed her Mazda. The waves were crashing high and strong that day. First, she filled her music bag with the quartets they would be performing. Then she packed her suitcase with concert black skirts and velvet tops, a silk evening gown, comfortable travel clothes for the two women, and everything else they would need. She and Melissa wore the same size in almost everything. She added two pairs of jeans, colorful tops, and a few scarves. She opened the hatchback and loaded the cellos with sleeping bags on top of them. Then, she filled the rest of the car with her tent, two camping pads, two pillows, dried fruit, nuts and snacks.

When Melissa returned from swimming, Arianna had a travel lunch ready. A few minutes later, they were in the car and rolling. Mermaid and musician were wearing matching sunglasses with red frames as they drove down Route 1. They tossed melodies back and forth as they were driving, mainly Appalachian fiddle tunes. Arianna was in a celebratory mood. She told Melissa, "This was what we did every summer with my family when I was growing up." Inside, she knew it might be Melissa's last adventure in a world that was still strange to her, and she wanted to make it a good one. She was also stretching her time with Melissa, who had become her closest friend.

The women in the quartet were hosted in San Francisco at the home of friends who lived in a Bernard Maybeck house in the Marina District. Along with the Palace of Fine Arts, Maybeck had designed several homes in their neighborhood. Many of their windows had an unobstructed view of the Bay. Since their children were grown, they had enough guest rooms for the whole group, and they loved hearing the rehearsals. Jeffrey and Suzanne owned a winery in Sonoma, and Suzanne was a gourmet cook. For dinner, she served salmon glazed with a honey walnut sauce; herbed sweet potatoes; a salad of arugula, heirloom tomatoes, mozzarella and figs; creamery butter and sourdough bread. Arianna and Melissa shared a room with a view of Angel Island, Alcatraz, and the Golden Gate Bridge. After the rehearsal, Suzanne served a custard fruit tart, topped with strawberries, blueberries, kiwi, and slices of mango. She set out an assortment of herbal teas with her grandmother's tea set on a silver tray. Amelia, who played viola and served as publicist for the group, let their hosts know that she had reserved comp tickets for them in a box close to the stage at the Herbst Theatre.

Further north, Jeremy stayed for two days with his

friend from the Santa Rosa Symphony. He was trying to clear his head as he listened to the different voices swirling inside him. He practiced Copland and Gershwin for an upcoming concert – *Appalachian Spring* and *Rhapsody in Blue*. After a three hour rehearsal, he bought a burrito, ate lunch, and began to drive home. He walked in Armstrong Woods in an attempt to calm himself, but he was agitated as he drove up the coast. He wasn't sure how he would feel when he got back home or what he would say to Melissa.

When he arrived at the cabin, it was empty. No note. No cellos. Nobody home. He made himself dinner and stayed overnight. All night, he tossed between edgy dreams, with the ocean crashing on the cliffs.

Chapter 48:
The Late Beethoven Quartets

*T*heir first concert was at the Herbst Theatre in San Francisco, with a program of late Beethoven quartets. Amelia always introduced the program, as Arianna and both violinists tended to be nonverbal before they played. Amelia explained, "We were all smitten with the late Beethoven Quartets at Julliard, but I later discovered that I needed more life experience to understand them. They ask a lot of the musicians, both technically and emotionally. The late quartets went far beyond the comprehension of musicians and audiences of his time but are now widely considered to be among the greatest musical compositions of all time.

"Playing this music is like climbing Mt. Everest. The late quartets are immensely difficult, and for many musicians, it's a life-long journey. Many people try to climb Everest and they die. They've given everything in their lives to do this. Very few reach the top. Keep in mind, Beethoven was totally deaf when he wrote these quartets. They come from another plane. His health was failing and he had one foot in the afterlife. The man was totally in his imagination, in another world, another universe. When we play these pieces, we're with him in the paradise of his imagination. I hope you listen that way.

"We're going to start with *Opus 130 in B-flat Major*. The great astronomer, Carl Sagan, chose the *Cavetina* from this quartet for the golden record carried on the Voyager spacecraft, and he asked to have it played at his memorial in the Cathedral of St. John the Divine in New York. He felt this piece represented one of the greatest achievements of life on Earth, and he hoped that one day another intelligent civilization might have the opportunity to hear it. At this concert, we invite you to travel in space and time with us. After the break, we'll play *Opus 131 in C sharp minor*."

The lights went down and there was a hush in the theatre. The musicians took a breath in unison and then began the *Adagio ma non troppo*. As she listened, Melissa traveled in time and moved between earth and water. Everything kept shifting. *Presto*. She knew she was at the edge of another world, and the music was asking her to take a huge leap. *Andante con moto*. She was smitten with Beethoven and could never fully enter his mysteries. *Allegro assai*. She swam inside a torrent of notes and emotion. *Cavatina*. *Adagio molto espressivo*. Melissa was still trying to figure out what it meant to be human. *Grosse Fuga*. It felt like an invisible bridge she could not cross.

After the concert Melissa met Arianna backstage. Quartet and mermaid took a taxi to Chinatown for dinner and enjoyed a feast of hot and sour soup, vegetarian pot stickers, mu shu with prawns and vegetables, eggplant with spicy garlic sauce, string beans a la Hunan, and tofu asparagus in black bean sauce. At the end of the meal, the waiter brought a plate of sliced oranges and fortune cookies, which the musicians took turns reading out loud.

"You will meet a tall dark stranger on an enchanted, musical evening."

"You are well-liked by many people and will live a long, musical life."

"You will take a ride into the sky on a Ferris wheel on the Santa Monica Pier." Lots of giggles around the table.

"You will cross the great ocean and play string quartets in Paris."

"Your mother will come to your next concert." Melissa wasn't sure if they were reading the fortunes from the cookies or improvising.

Two days later, they played a concert at UC Santa Cruz, with a matinee the next day at Cabrillo College. The Santa Cruz campus was built in a forest of redwood trees. The music program had its major focus on Western classical music but also incorporated the study of ethnic and world music, including various folk traditions and jazz. While in Santa Cruz, Arianna spoke to an American music class about growing up on Signal Mountain and the tradition of fiddle tunes in the Appalachian Mountains. She told stories about the Mountain Opry and played a few fiddle tunes on the cello. Later, she went with Melissa and a few students to the Santa Cruz Beach Boardwalk to eat ice cream and ride the world famous Giant Dipper roller coaster. It's one of the oldest wooden roller coasters in the world and survived the Loma Prieta earthquake, although they shut it down for a month to check every nail and bolt. Melissa was amazed and amused at what humans do to enjoy themselves. Riding the roller coaster reminded her of mermaid children taking rides on ocean currents, never thinking of how far their parents would need to search to find them.

Their next stop was a small concert hall in Cambria, run by a gypsy fiddler with an earlier career as concertmaster of three orchestras. Like many classically trained folk musicians, Brynne had reached a point where she realized that improvising and composing gave her more joy than playing music written by other people. She liked the freedom of messing with the melody and adding unexpected harmonies. When her father suddenly needed more care than she could give as a traveling musician, she made a major life change and helped restore a historic chapel for use as a concert hall. It was now a coveted venue for touring classical and folk musicians.

The program in Cambria included a late Beethoven quartet, a Brahms quartet, and a quartet by Matthew Arnerich. The composer drove down the coast with his wife and infant daughter to give the preconcert talk. For dinner, Brynne reserved a table at the Black Cat Bistro. After a leisurely meal and two shared desserts, the musicians spent the night at a bed and breakfast. Arianna and Melissa shared a room with twin beds and Victorian fairy decor. As they slept, fairies flew into the room and sang to them.

Traveling down the coast, Arianna pulled over often to enjoy lookouts with views of the ocean. They watched the coast change as they moved further south. In Santa Barbara, the ocean was warmer, and Melissa had never seen so many palm trees. She went for a swim and then watched surfers riding waves. Some of their antics reminded her of dolphins. Further south, they pulled over at sunset to watch the ocean of sky change colors, reflected on the water. That night, they were hosted by a poet friend in Ventura. Mary Kay had a condo so close to the beach they could hear the waves crash while they were sleeping. Her walls were full of art and photographs that told stories. Since Mary Kay loved Bach, Arianna played the Second Unaccompanied Cello Suite for her. She was delighted to hear it in her living room.

Melissa felt that chamber music was more intimate than an orchestra. She could savor and separate the sounds while enjoying how they wove together. Their next concert was at the Greystone Mansion and Gardens in Beverly Hills, a Tudor mansion surrounded by formal English gardens. The program included quartets by Beethoven, Brahms and Shostakovich, followed by a meet the artists champagne reception and a tour of the mansion. The women in the quartet wore matching purple silk evening gowns, and their concert received a rave review in the *Los Angeles Times*.

After the concert, they changed clothes and went to the Santa Monica Pier. Arianna was always careful to bring Melissa close to their destination to make sure she didn't have to do a lot of walking. They sat on a bench, watching a parade of locals and tourists, and then they rode the carousel. Later, they met friends at the Inn of the Seventh Ray in Topanga Canyon, where they shared a meal of charred leek and potato soup, roasted mushroom toast with sherry tarragon cream, and a creamy truffle risotto. Melissa was charmed by the tiny lights above the tables. They reminded her of the filtered light under the ocean. She started thinking about her home again and her growing desire to return there. They stayed that night with their friends in Topanga Canyon, and Melissa's dreams had tiny lights underwater, guiding her as she swam with tropical fish into coral caves.

The next morning, the quartet played a matinee at Santa Monica Catholic Church. They arrived two hours early to set up and practice, then played another concert of late Beethoven quartets. The concert ended an hour before a wedding, and by prior arrangement, they stayed to play music for the bride and groom as their guests arrived. Melissa had never seen a wedding, so Arianna took her upstairs to watch the celebration from the balcony. Melissa was fascinated by the ceremony and what it meant to the couple getting married. The bride wore a vintage mermaid style lace wedding gown, form fitting at the bodice and waist with a flared skirt. The groom wore a white tuxedo with a hot pink satin cummerbund and bow tie, and the priest spoke beautiful words as he blessed them.

That night, they stayed with musician friends in Manhattan Beach. Before bed, Melissa told Arianna how much she loved the ceremony and asked, "Do you think your brother will ever have a wedding?"

Arianna rolled her eyes and sighed, "Who knows?"

Chapter 49:

Energy Circles in Sedona

*T*hey played the final concert of their tour at the Athenaeum Music and Arts Library in La Jolla – a warm and intimate setting for music. At the request of their hosts, the concert was a celebration of female composers. During the first half of the concert, two members of the quartet were joined by a mezzo soprano and a pianist for the *Piano Trio in G Minor* by Clara Schumann and two of her concert songs. After intermission, the quartet performed the *Fifth String Quartet* by Dmitri Shostakovich because he used musical themes by Galina Ustvolskaya, who was his student. When Amelia introduced the quartet, the musicians played a few of her themes so the audience would know what to listen for. Their final piece was the *String Quartet in G Major* by African American composer Florence Price. Her music was full of incandescent textures that called early Hollywood to mind. After resounding applause and an encore, the musicians mingled with the guests at a wine and cheese reception in the foyer.

They stayed that night with a patron of the arts in San Diego, a retired cellist who was delighted to have more time with the musicians. Lenore's hands were too arthritic to continue playing, but she loved talking about music. Earlier in her life, she had enjoyed a career in Paris and Sweden, playing chamber music and performing with European orchestras. She was smitten with all of the music on the program that afternoon and shared memories of playing music by Clara Schumann in Paris. On a tour of Russia, she met Galina Ustvolskaya, played music with her, and was inspired to champion her music. Lenore regretted that Galina was ignored by the Soviets, but she received the recognition she deserved outside of the USSR.

After a round of sparkling Martinelli's cider, Lenore served a Mexican-themed dinner buffet to her guests. They continued to talk about music in the afterglow of their concert tour. Most of the quartet would be heading north in the morning, but Arianna and Melissa had other plans.

"I'm taking Melissa on a little vacation. Believe it or not, she's never been out of California." Well, that wasn't exactly true, but it avoided a tumble of questions.

"How long are you going to be away?"

"We have ten days before I have to be back to rehearse for our next concert, and perhaps we can stretch it to twelve. Amelia, what do you think?"

"I could use a vacation too. Our concert today was quite a workout, not our usual repertoire."

"Do you want to join us? You'd have to buy a tent . . ."

"I'd love to, but I have theatre tickets on Monday night in San Francisco, and on Tuesday, I have a full schedule of students at the Conservatory."

"Well, maybe another time. When I was growing up, my family did a road trip every summer. We'd plan it months in advance." Arianna smiled.

"Where will you be going?"

"Sedona first. I have a friend from Julliard who lives there, and she invited us to stay for a few days. From there, we'll drive to the Grand Canyon. I have other places planned but I'm leaving room to be spontaneous. Some nights, we'll be camping and other nights staying with friends. I have sleeping bags and a tent in the back of the car."

"Do you want me to take your music and concert clothes back to San Francisco?"

"That would be sweet."

"And what about your cellos? I'm sure you don't want to take them across the desert!"

"I was planning to leave them with Lenore in San Diego, but if you can bring them back to San Francisco, we'll be able to travel back to Anchor Bay from Tahoe at the end of our vacation instead of taking a Southern route."

"No problem."

Melissa looked disappointed. She said softly to Arianna, "But I was hoping to play with you while we travel."

"It's too much of a risk. Cellos can be terribly damaged by sunlight and heat, but we can borrow a cello in Sedona."

"No duets?"

"My friend Beth is a pianist. She can play duets with you."

In the morning at Lenore's insistence, they all went to the San Diego Zoo. Melissa loved the flowers and the pandas. She was fascinated to see animals from other parts of the world. Lenore asked them to join her for a Thai lunch at a local café before returning home. Then, fueled by a good meal, a tall glass of Thai iced tea, and two chocolate truffles, Arianna and Melissa started driving through the desert.

Arianna was elated to be traveling again in the style of the family vacations from her childhood, and Melissa traveled in a state of wide-eyed wonder. She loved watching the land change and thought about different textures of ocean. She was fascinated by the various species of cacti and their ability to survive with a minimum of water. Tumbleweed was another amazement, along with the clear blue of the desert sky. Lenore had packed fruit and sandwiches for them so they could arrive in Sedona before dark. As they got closer, both women began to feel the majesty and the power of the red rock cliffs.

Arianna's friend Beth lived in an adobe house and played piano with a trio in Sedona. She also accompanied classical singers and visiting musicians. Over dinner, she told Melissa about the vortex locations and explained that they were powerful places to receive energy from the Earth. "When I meditate in these places, I go deep inside myself and feel connected with every atom in the universe. My mind is filled with energy and light."

Melissa, tired of pretending she wasn't a mermaid, told Beth that the red rock cliffs they saw as they were driving into Sedona look like cliffs under the sea.

Beth, without asking how she knew this, smiled. "Sedona used to be an ocean. Now she is a dried up ocean, and we all get to live here."

Melissa's eyes lit up.

In the morning, Beth took them on a tour of Sedona, since she knew where to find the vortexes and the best places to view the red rock cliffs. At the Cathedral Rock Vortex – the place that felt right to both of them – Arianna and Melissa began to chant and improvise. Melissa sang music from the ocean, and Arianna added a layer of harmony. The music sent shivers up Beth's spine, and she toned with them in her sweet mezzo-soprano voice. Beth asked them to meditate with her. She began to hum softly and they entered a deep silence.

Melissa was surprised that humans knew how to feel what she was feeling now. First a sense of floating. Then waves of energy and light. She knew that Beth and Arianna were floating in the same waves, going deeper and deeper. Subtle levels of creation became visible, layer after layer, like a dream flower opening.

In that long, transparent moment, they reached a place so deep that the mermaid and human worlds flowed into one another and embraced. They floated in a world beyond time, where the atoms in the core of stars and the cellular memory of the heart are one. As images revealed themselves, the mysteries of creation became transparent. The walls between species dissolved, along with the barriers of space and time.

The visions of astronomers, the mysteries of music, and the secrets of astrophysics floated in a silent unity.

The desires of the heart, the brilliance of the mind, and the urgings of the creative spirit merged in the core of all being. Everything was lit from within.

Mermaid and musicians floated in the mysteries. Looking back, they never knew how long, but gradually, they floated back to the world they knew, passing through layer after layer of creation. Everything was full of light.

They sat in silence for a while, the waves of the other world still washing over them. Beth began to hum, in resonance with the hum of the Earth. Arianna joined the hum with a harmony and Melissa added a descant of ocean sounds. Their music rose, flew like birds of light and circled back. Beth opened her backpack, spread out a Navajo blanket, and offered food to her friends – cranberry walnut bread, wedges of cheese, a bowl of figs, a jar of artichoke hearts, and a bowl of Pinot Noir grapes. She opened a bottle of pressed cider and invited her friends to eat and drink. The food invited them to return to their bodies, to the moment, to the earth.

After eating, they continued their tour of red rocks and other vortexes. At the Boynton Canyon Vortex, Arianna and Beth improvised a vocal duet with passages from Bach. Clearly, Bach was a composer who knew the mysteries. Arianna shared her memory of a Bach concert when she was a student at Julliard. "On Bach's birthday, we played a marathon concert with students and audience migrating in and out of the auditorium. It began with an organ student performing the Toccata and Fugue in D Minor, followed by a few motets. Then the orchestra walked on stage to play the Second Brandenburg Concerto, the Concerto for Two Harpsichords, and the Concerto for Three Harpsichords. Just after sunset, five soloists and the Julliard Opera Chorus joined us to sing the Magnificat."

Beth added her memories. "It was our third year at Julliard, and I played the harpsichord concertos."

"During the last two hours of the concert, I began to feel the presence of J.S. Bach, and the feeling kept getting stronger. By the time we played the Magnificat, I was sure that the Maestro was there, listening and playing with us."

"As I was playing the Concerto for Two Harpsichords, it felt like Bach was playing with me, adding harmonies and embellishments. I know there was another student playing the harpsichord, but from a deep place inside me, it felt like the Maestro. I could feel him smiling as I played."

"Exactly, and it wasn't just an idea. It was him. On the stage, we were playing the Magnificat. Inside, we were flying in other-worldly ecstasy. Since that concert, one of my private pleasures is playing the Bach Cello Suites late at night, with no one listening. And sometimes, by the ocean with the moon glowing on my cello, the old man whispers to me."

Melissa was understanding more and more what it felt like and what it meant to be a musician. That night, the cellist and violinist from Beth's trio came for dessert – strawberry shortcake and then a Brahms trio they had been rehearsing. After an encore, they went outside to admire the Milky Way in the desert sky. Then it was time to dream.

In the morning, they drove to the Grand Canyon. Arianna was careful to make sure that Melissa would not have to walk beyond her comfort zone, but they hiked a bit along the rim of the canyon. Beth explained that the layered bands of rock revealed millions of years of geological history. Years ago, she had rafted down the Colorado River.

At a gift shop, Arianna found a slice of agate she wanted to take home, and she asked Melissa if she wanted something. Melissa looked at the geodes, which reminded her of ocean caves. She picked up an amethyst geode and put it down again.

Arianna watched and saw that it was a beautiful stone. She asked Melissa if she'd like to keep it.

Melissa said quietly, "I can't take it with me."

What they didn't talk about – both of them knew they would be parting company soon. It gave the whole adventure a sense of nostalgia, even while it was happening. While Melissa was in the rest room, Arianna purchased the geode and quietly slipped it into her purse.

They drove back to Sedona for the evening and left early in the morning. Arianna and Melissa camped the rest of the time and traveled to Santa Fe, Taos, Chaco Canyon, Bryce Canyon, Yosemite and Lake Tahoe. They met people from all over the world. Each day held an amazement of small miracles. Melissa loved canyons because their geography was so similar to the world underwater. They had chosen the route together because of Melissa's love of canyons.

At a campground near Lake Tahoe, Arianna asked her friend, "I know we don't have time now, but do you want to see New York?"

Melissa got quiet and said, "I don't think so. Too many people. I was there when the Towers fell and there was nothing we could do to help. Anyhow, I need to talk with Jeremy."

"I wish I could to take you to Signal Mountain where I grew up."

Melissa quietly said, "It's time to go back now."

During the day, she forgot about Jeremy, but at night she was haunted by dreams. The worst part was she knew that what she was dreaming was true. Her grandmothers held counsel underwater and swam into her dreams. Every morning, she brushed salt and shells from her hair and face.

Arianna and Melissa took a boat ride around Lake Tahoe. The lake was a moving tapestry of gently reflected light as they swam in Emerald Bay. Now, they had one more night of camping under the stars before driving back to Anchor Bay. Without lights from a city, the Milky Way spread across the sky. It had been like that so many nights on Signal Mountain when she was growing up. But now, it was time for Arianna to prepare for her next concert, and Melissa had a swim team to prepare for the Olympics.

Chapter 50:

The Prophesy Stones

*U*nder the stars that night, six of Melissa's grandmothers appeared to her in a dream. They swam
to where she was sleeping and carried the six prophesy
stones on the outstretched palms of their hands. Their
long hair shimmered around them in the water. The
stones were smooth, round, and translucent – embedded
with precious and semi-precious stones. When joined
together, they formed a larger stone – a milky moonstone
where visions of the future appeared.

Grandmother Serafina, the one who had rescued the
little boy and then lived with his father on Bali, began the
conversation. "We've been watching you every day, and
there are events about to unfold that you need to be aware
of."

Her sister, Grandmother Sea Forest, continued. "We

always worry when a mermaid stays too long above the water, but we know how deeply you longed to be there."

Grandmother Angelina spoke. "There were times we were not able to reach you and did not know if you would return. But now, the sea tunnel has opened again. It will be your choice."

Grandmother Sophia shared her wisdom. "The future is fluid, as you learned when you were growing. When we put the stones together, you will see the possibilities."

Grandmother Persephone advised, "Choose wisely, dear one."

Grandmother Astarte gave her blessing. "We love you. Now, we will prepare the stones."

The mermaids sat in a circle, swaying like seaweed in tropical water. One by one, they extended their hands until the stones touched. The stones emitted a soft glow. Then an aura of warm light circled the stones and the mermaids who sat around them. The light inside the stones intensified and merged until they formed a single stone with milky visions. The visions were covered with seaweed, but as they watched, the place where the stones touched became clearer. With each wave of seawater, more and more was revealed.

Melissa watched the visions appear, one by one. They showed her six possible journeys that could become her life – with events, details and emotions. Six choices leading to six different futures. Her grandmothers were silent. They trusted that Melissa would know what to do. It would not be easy, but she knew.

Her grandmothers began to chant, and Melissa joined

them. Songs she had been singing with them for so many years. Then, one by one, they took the stones out of the circle and swam away. Melissa continued dreaming under the pearl light of the moon.

Chapter 51:

A Tango by Piazzolla

Jeremy and Tanya met in Cotati for another tango lesson. Tanya wore a purple satin dress, embellished with purple beads that caught the light like tiny stars. In her hair, a purple satin rose, and purple high-heeled dance shoes on her feet. The heels accentuated the muscles in her legs.

During the break, Jeremy went up to talk with the band. When they walked out to start the second set, Jeremy came up to the stage with his violin. He had prepared a surprise for Tanya and everyone else in the room – an Astor Piazzolla tango he played with passion and flair. Tanya was thrilled. She was mesmerized. She was smitten.

They danced until midnight and then drove back to Lagunitas. Another love night, another way to tango.

Again, he woke up with music, the echo of a mermaid, a quiet whispering in the overtones.

Tanya was intoxicated with her new love and hoping they might have a future together. That he wanted to be a father spoke to something deep inside her womb. A memory awakening. This was something she had wanted for so many years, something primal in her heart that had been smothered with disappointment. In the intensity of their loving, her body was speaking to her heart, releasing light that had been hidden inside the bark of a tree that had covered her emotions and her secret longings.

Jeremy wrote the music he heard and then played it for her, even though its source was somewhere else. Then he became very quiet.

She studied his face. "The mermaid again?"

He nodded.

"Just remember, you have dreamed this. You are telling me a story."

"I'm going to have to figure this out."

"And hopefully soon. The myth of the mermaid has always been mysterious, but I think you will find the solid earth more welcoming."

"Exactly. I'm glad you understand."

"Come outside now. I went to the greenhouse yesterday and have seedlings ready for planting. Some early tomatoes, arugula, marigolds and rudbeckia."

"Where I come from, they call them Black-eyed Susans. They grow wild by the side of the road in the mountains."

"Good memories then."

"You'll have to come with me to Signal Mountain one

day. I want you to see where I grew up – the trails, the flowers, the birds, my school, and the Mountain Opry."

"I would love that!"

Planting tomatoes distracted both of them from the issues at hand. Tanya had no idea what his life had been like before she met him. She didn't understand what he had tried to share with her, and he knew it. Clearly, there were parts of himself he could not reveal to Tanya. There were other parts of his life he could not share with Melissa. The future was inviting and confusing. At some point he would have to come to terms with all of this, probably soon.

Based in Lagunitas, it would be easier to get to rehearsals of the Santa Rosa Symphony. This would provide a good excuse for being away. The new season was starting soon, and he never drove home at night after rehearsals.

Tanya was not a soulmate, even though she was sexy and delightful, but she was human. He felt he needed that.

Chapter 52:
The Firefly

*T*wo weeks after they returned to Anchor Bay, Melissa traveled with her team to the Olympics. She let Celeste take the lead, and although she was not quite at the level of her teacher, her performance was stunning. Melissa sat on the bench reserved for the team coach and manager, delighting in the beauty of the mermaid water ballet and the way it reminded her of her home in the ocean. If they won, she wanted to give the celebrity to Celeste, knowing how her performance that day would create her future. It would also shield Melissa from a barrage of questions she would not be able to answer.

Jeremy and Arianna borrowed a TV and watched from Anchor Bay. The performance of the Russian team was an edgy hip hop piece – danced with the precision of the Bolshoi Ballet. The Japanese team swam inside a silhouette of a temple in Kyoto, with costumes styled in the Kabuki tradition and music of taiko drums and temple bells. Yes, they expected serious competition – you don't get to the Olympics without performing at the level of mastery. The final water ballet was Melissa's choreography, performed by the Mermaids of Team USA.

From the first note of the music and opening movements of the water dance, everyone entered the sacred circle of mermaids. The corps de ballet of mermaids moved in svelte synchronized patterns, swimming like dolphins in shapes dissolving and changing as they swam. Their costumes sparkled in emerald green, with soft sequins from shoulders to mermaid tail. Their lithe beauty felt like a vision from somewhere back in time. Like Melissa, Celeste entered the water with a backflip and sideways spin, twisting herself in the air and arching her back as she entered the water. Her movements created a story ballet as a stunning kaleidoscope of grace and power. Celeste added a subtle sensuality to the moves Melissa taught her, and as she swam, the audience felt like they were really seeing a mermaid. The corps de ballet mirrored her sensuality, enhanced by the music full of ancient mermaid songs. After her solo, she joined the other mermaids and swam with them as music became movement. Their tails submerged and reappeared before the final cadenza, waves of beauty until the final shimmering notes. Then a splash and graceful exit swim to the side of the pool.

Now, the scores and the announcement of the winners. Team USA scored a perfect ten – gold medals for the Mermaids. What a celebration! The women on the team were hugging each other and hugging Melissa. Halfway around the world, Jeremy and Arianna jumped up, cheered and hugged each other.

Melissa stayed with her team to celebrate and then travel for a while. It was an opportunity to see more of the world, to enjoy the food of other countries, and to speak other languages. Wherever they went, she was able to translate. If a teammate asked her how she learned the language, she just smiled and said, "I've done a bit of travel in my time."

In September, the Santa Rosa Symphony began rehearsals. Now, Jeremy stayed in Lagunitas after he danced or played a concert. Melissa was still traveling, and Arianna never asked him questions. His tango woman was a vine, a tree, a butterfly. Beautiful curves, like mountains and rivers. Jeremy was enchanted and tried not to think of the lovely mermaid he had left behind. When he played the violin for Tanya, he didn't listen to the quiet whispering in the overtones.

During those weeks of timeless time, it became even more clear that he wanted to be a father. This was something his new love wanted too, something she could give him. Around them, a new soul started flickering, something like a firefly. A musical being who wanted to come back to the world.

One night after the season changed, a dream of a mermaid flashed across Jeremy's eyes while he was sleeping. A river of pearls and a kiss across the water. Then a melody in a minor key. In the morning, he knew he had to travel north again. Melissa would be returning soon. A few days later, he returned to the cabin by the cove, unsure of what he would say when he arrived.

Chapter 53:
The Night of Shooting Stars

*M*elissa and Jeremy sat on the deck, watching meteor showers fly across the sky in the dark dark night. Finding the right words was not a problem because Melissa had already dreamed everything. All he could do was take out his violin and play for her. He poured his emotions into the music. There was nothing he could tell her because she already knew. All of it. Mermaids have the gift of prophesy. And yes, she had been told by her grandmothers that humans were this way. They cannot become like you, and you cannot become like them. In time, they will always disappoint.

Jeremy held her in his arms and said, "I hope you can understand." Yes, she understood too well. He was the one who did not know how powerfully her tears were pulling her back to the ocean. They talked for hours, holding each other. "You are the reason," he told her, "that I am not afraid of love. Your love has freed me in a way that no earth woman could."

"Then why didn't you stay?" She spoke softly as she gazed into his eyes. "Earth women will always disappoint you."

"I've been wrestling with my emotions for months, but one thing I know. I will always love you."

"Then why are you leaving?"

"What I came to know, while I was struggling with my feelings, is that I long to be the father to a child. A human child. That child is already on the way."

"I saw that in a dream. Are you going to have a wedding?"

Jeremy hesitated. "I'm still wrestling with my emotions, but it's the right thing to do. Human children need a stable family to feel loved."

"In a church?"

"No, just a small ceremony with Tanya's parents, her sister, and a few friends – not like the wedding you saw with my sister. We'll be married inside a grove of redwood trees."

A cloud passed over Melissa's eyes and then dissolved. "What about the Grandmothers?"

"Humans don't live as long as Mer people. My son will have one grandmother, and both of my parents speak to me in my dreams. They come often now. After my son is born, I will play him the fiddle tunes my father played for me when we were living on Signal Mountain."

Melissa smiled. "I hope you know he is one of your Guardian Angels."

"That must be why I see him so often when I am sleeping. A few days ago, I saw him holding the baby in one of my dreams."

Melissa closed her eyes. "The name I hear from the soul is Firefly."

They sat on the deck, under the stars, listening to waves crash against the cliffs. They were silent, wrapped around each other. Their love glowed around them like a pearl of moonlight. It was pure and bright.

"The prophesy stones showed me what you are telling me now."

"It was just too much of a risk, not knowing if you would have to take our baby back into the water. To lose both of you at the same time would be more than I could bear. I would have gone into a very dark place, and I'm not sure I would have found my way out."

"I saw that in the stones. Our child would have been Mer, and before she was born, I would have had to return to the water. Mermaid children are always born in the water."

"My father came to me in a dream and asked me to bring the music I learned on Signal Mountain to a new generation of musicians. He's afraid the music will get lost unless the fiddlers from the Appalachian Mountains find a way to share their music with young musicians from other places."

"The new soul who is coming to you is a musician. I know that from the stones."

Holding each other in loving embrace, he gazed at her, lost in the ocean of her eyes. His hands were trembling. He felt the tremendous gift he had been given, time out of time, a journey into a mysterious world that he was tossing back into the sea. With tears in his eyes, he whispered, "You will always be a part of me."

Melissa spoke again. "Jeremy, I want you to have that child, your little Firefly. It's a beautiful name and the one his soul has chosen. I will be – what do you call it? Auntie. As he grows, I will come into his dreams."

Slowly, sadly, he got up to leave. He walked to the door of the cabin, then came back to her, hugged her long and hard. Gave her long, lingering kisses. Pulled her close again and again. Further south, a firefly was calling, circling around his shoulders. Filling his heart with a tiny, flickering light.

Melissa knew what she would do in the morning, but she kept silence.

Chapter 54:

What the Moon Whispered

*A*rianna took out her cello and played Bach, what she did when she wanted to express herself but the words were silent. The key was D Minor, the Second Bach Unaccompanied Cello Suite. She played it for her sister. As she listened to everything Melissa shared, she kept saying, "This is not what I expected. I am so disappointed in my brother." Rain was pouring down the window, making tides and rivers on the glass. Later, the clouds blew out to sea, and again the moonlight floated on the water in the cove. The Pacific Ocean roared in the distance, with dolphins swimming in currents away from shore.

Sea sister and earth sister talked long into the night. Arianna brewed two cups of chamomile tea with honey and served them with blueberry muffins. Ten roses stretching from Rosa's Murano glass vase caught the moonlight on their petals. The two women talked about everything earth, sea and sky. Love, music and betrayal. A shower of falling stars. What the moon whispered. Earth wisdom and secrets in the water.

Arianna gazed at her sister, her eyes glazed with tears. She told her about a dream she remembered from a few nights ago, a man with blue eyes and curly hair. She had a feeling she would meet him.

Melissa affirmed. "The angels have been whispering to you. He's the one you have been waiting for, the one your soul has chosen. Like you, he is a very musical being. Pay attention to the mermaids in your dreams and listen to your intuition. You will meet him soon."

"I'm really sorry about my brother. I know he loved you deeply."

"It's different up here. Under the sea, love is constant. Up here, love can change over time, twist like a water snake, molt like a cicada, and take another form."

The rain started again, then stopped for a while, as it does during early winter storms. Melissa walked out to the deck, watched the full moon rippling the water in Anchor Bay. Memories of music flooded her, memories of the way he had loved her. She thought about what she loved in the world of the humans – dragonflies, birds, music, fields of flowers, redwood trees. The gift of three amazing years. She walked back inside, poured tea into both cups, and the women kept talking.

Mainly, Arianna listened. At one point she gazed at Melissa, and said, "Love doesn't just die – it gets murdered."

Melissa's eyes grew narrow, then opened again. She spoke slowly. "You will have to forgive him. He's your brother."

Chapter 55:

To the Shimmering Ocean

Just before dawn in a mermaid dream, Melissa heard her grandmothers whispering. Her mermaid world had blended with the human, but now her mermaid tears were pulling her back to sea.

Her dream went back in time, to an earlier century in the human world. It felt like looking through a window. *Five minutes past midnight. Night before the full moon.* But who was she seeing?

She finishes stitching purple yarn through an old grey hat. But who was this woman? Who made the handloom leaning against her wall? Someone's grandmother in her younger years? *He has been watching*, but where did he come from? A musician or a sailor? And who is he, really?

By the window, a candle was burning. *The wax is dull yellow. Flames flash on the Persian rug.* Where did he come from? Where is he going? *His body assumes the rhythm of a Pinter play. In a mirror, she takes the form of the highest strains of Shostakovich. He looks into her eyes, only to see the snow of earlier winters.*

The human world – what a twisted marble! An agate flying through space. A multi-layered history of music, tears and joy inside an expanding universe.

Time expanded and condensed. She heard the music of the great romantic composers. Beethoven's Ninth Symphony. Brahms' *Requiem*. Mozart's piano concertos. Outside the window, a wolf moon falling into the Pacific. A rainbow around the moon, sky ballet. Inside the window, a sky of dreams, visions becoming music. Beethoven's *Moonlight Sonata*. Poulenc's *Gloria*. Tchaikovsky's *Swan Lake*. The events of the past few weeks, the *Pathetique Symphony*, the *Firebird* – ballerinas off stage, waiting for a dream. Bees ready to swarm. Tectonic plates rumbling.

She thought of Jeremy and felt the betrayal in her fins, as she began to remember them. Her fins were pulling her back to the ocean, where waves and salt would wash her memories.

Just before sunrise, the ocean reached into her dreams, speaking to her in waves of traveling light. The sound of cicadas flying from a distance, a profusion of butterflies lifting from coastal eucalyptus trees. The moon whispering. It was time for Melissa to return to the sea, and she did not hesitate. She did not think about the life she was leaving or the man she had loved. The ocean was calling. With the full moon shining on the water, she walked to the beach by Anchor Bay. Down the long trail, past lavender, manzanita, California poppies, and poison oak. Along the beach, shining with shells, stones and sea glass. As she walked to the water, she shed her clothes, like prayer flags in the wind. A green silk blouse, an ocean blue Indian skirt, a lavender camisole.

Her legs were shimmering, turning silver. With each step closer to the waves, the shimmering intensified. As her toes touched the water and the waves embraced her, her skin transformed into a rainbow. The ocean was singing, first a salty tune, then a haunting symphony. Deeper into the water, her mermaid tail became less of an afterimage, then lucid with silver. Memories of her time on the land filled with waves, filled with water. She had returned to the sea, back to her own people. Once again, she was free.

As she returned to the sea, thousands of tiny fish swirled around her in watery embrace. Lantern fish lit her way as she swam deeper and deeper into the ocean. Forests of coral, kelp and sea anemones waved in the current.

The transformation to mermaid was ecstatic. Gills revealing an ancient way of breathing. Her mermaid tail, emerald and silver.

She swam deeper and deeper, back to her own, where the circle of mermaids was waiting. "Welcome home," they sang to her in the Mer language. Yes, this was home.

She felt pure joy as the water embraced her. The sky was a rainbow – turquoise light filtered through the ocean, eternal and shimmering. And since she was not human, the life she had left behind became more and more like a dream.

About the Author

Diane Frank is author of eight books of poems, three novels, and a photo memoir of her 400 mile trek in the Nepal Himalayas. *While Listening to the Enigma Variations: New and Selected Poems* won the 2022 Next Generation Indie Book Award for Poetry. She is also editor of three bestselling anthologies: *River of Earth and Sky: Poems for the Twenty-First Century*; *Fog and Light: San Francisco through the Eyes of the Poets Who Live Here*; and *Pandemic Puzzle Poems*. Diane teaches at San Francisco State University and Dominican University of San Rafael. She played cello with the Golden Gate Symphony for eighteen years and collaborated with Matt Arnerich as he composed an orchestral suite based on her poem, "Tree of Life." *Blackberries in the Dream House*, her first novel, won the Chelson Award for Fiction and was nominated for the Pulitzer Prize. Her photo memoir, *Letters from a Sacred Mountain Place: A Journey through the Nepal Himalayas*, invites you into the magic of the mountains with stories, poems and 53 full-page color photographs.

To schedule readings, book signings and workshops, and to invite her to speak to your book club, contact:

E-mail: GeishaPoet@aol.com
Website: www.dianefrank.com

Books by Diane Frank

Mermaids and Musicians

While Listening to the Enigma Variations: New and Selected
    Poems

Letters from a Sacred Mountain Place: A Journey through the
    Nepal Himalayas

Canon for Bears and Ponderosa Pines

Yoga of the Impossible

Blackberries in the Dream House

Swan Light

Entering the Word Temple

The Winter Life of Shooting Stars

The All Night Yemenite Café

Rhododendron Shedding Its Skin

Isis: Poems by Diane Frank

Anthologies

River of Earth and Sky: Poems for the Twenty-First Century
    (Editor)

Fog and Light: San Francisco through the Eyes of the Poets
    Who Live Here (Editor)

Pandemic Puzzle Poems (Co-editor)

Carrying the Branch: Poets in Search of Peace (Co-editor)

Eclipsed Moon Coins: Twenty-Six Visionary Poets (Editor)